BEHIND THE SMILE

BEHIND THE SMILE

A Novel

Based on a True Life Story

Dianne Nice

DB

DIADEM BOOKS

Published by Diadem Books

For information, please contact:

Diadem Books
Ocean Surf
CLASHNESSIE
IV27 4JF
Scotland UK

www.diadembooks.com

Cover design by Angus Muller

This is a work of fiction. Characters and situations are entirely a result of the author's imagination.

Some descriptive scenes may not be suitable for children.

ISBN: 978-0-9559741-5-1

Dedicated to all those who may feel that there is no hope for a better tomorrow!

Table of Contents

Chapters

Acknowledgements

I am indebted to my husband for his love and support, without which this book would never have existed!

Sincere thanks are also due to my friend Dr. Charles Muller, of Diadem Books, for his never-ending patience, constant encouragement, and invaluable assistance in completing this book.

Dianne Nice

Chapter One

From Pillar to Post

I stood looking at her lying in bed, reached out and pulled her eyelids back. Her eyes were brown. Nothing...I felt nothing. I pulled the covers back and looked at her body. One last look. She was dead! And I wanted to slap her! She was my mother. I had tried so hard to love her and make her love me. Now I couldn't shed a tear. Maybe I had cried too many tears because of her while she was alive.

My mother, Rita (Derline), and father Victor Gidney, were married on June 27, 1940, when she was nineteen years old. I was born on February 16, 1942, and given the name Laura Lillian (after my grandmother). My little sister Carmen was born on June 2, 1945.

My first memory is of being a little girl standing on a couch, hair in long ringlets, and reaching for a phone on the wall. I remember very little else except being pulled across the floor by my hair. That must have hurt—and who in the world would do that to any child? Maybe it's a good thing I don't remember much. No one ever told me stories about my young years though I did ask.

But I do remember the smell of ether. They were putting a mask on my face as I lay on a table. "What are they doing to me?" It was a question any little two-year-old girl would ask. The next thing I remember is waking up in a strange bed, in a strange room. There was a little girl in the bed beside mine and her face looked like someone had painted it all white. Had they painted my face white too? And why was my leg so hard to move? It was heavy. Where did that hard white bandage come from? It wasn't there before. I had so many questions but there was no one there to ask. I started to cry.

A nurse brought me something to eat and was angry at me for saying I didn't like porridge. I didn't like it but they didn't give me anything else, so I tried to eat it anyway. My right arm was weaker than my left one and it was hard to hold anything with my right hand. I was left-handed but maybe that was because my right hand wouldn't do what I wanted it to. Sometimes I was clumsy, they told me.

I remember the sound of a crash as I reached for something on a bedside table. I heard the nurse say, "You little brat! Look what a mess you made!" I guess she wasn't happy about that either. But what was a little girl to do with her leg in a cast? "You will stay in bed until I say you can get up."

After I went home, they told me I had polio. My grandmother Lillian looked after me when my mother and father went to work. Everybody called her "Lil". She used to sing me songs and I loved it when she sang "Rock-a-bye Baby", but I didn't like the part about the cradle falling.

Grammy Lil took me to the doctor to have my cast removed. I remember exclaiming when I looked at my leg: "Oh, it's so small!" The doctor said that was because it had been in a cast for so long—"It had atrophied," he said. I didn't know what that meant, but I guessed that meant it had got smaller. "Now you will have to wear a brace on your leg." The brace was made of steel and leather. It was heavy and when I tried to walk, it made a *clunk, clunk* sound. I didn't like it. People looked at me and said, "Oh what a sin!" *Was* it a sin?

Mom started to get very fat, and about a year later, my little sister Carmen was born. She would cry almost as loud as my mother hollered. Carmen was still a little baby when my daddy stopped coming home. I didn't see him again until I was five years old. He was a bus driver and stopped in to see me where I was living then. I sat on his lap and he taught me to whistle. We talked about Santa Claus. I don't remember what else happened, but I do know I never saw him or heard from him again until I was all grown up.

After my mother and father stopped living together, my younger sister Carmen and I were placed with our mother's sister Thelma, and her husband Hubert Belliveau, in a little French village called St. Bernard, on Nova Scotia's French Acadian shore. It was there that we learned to speak French—Acadian French. *Oui* was pronounced "way" and *Non* was pronounced "neigh-o". I could pronounce all the words but I sure couldn't spell them. Aunt Thelma had never learned to speak French. "You are not allowed to speak French when you are in this house," she told us. We always had to remember where we were.

Uncle Hubert had a little grocery store beside the house, and my sister and I would often play in there and scoop a handful of brown sugar out of a barrel when nobody was

3

looking. He also had big bags of what they called "feed" in the back room. Sometimes we would scoop a handful of that too but it didn't taste very good. It was food for cows. Uncle Hubert would deliver the feed to people on his half-ton truck and Carmen and I would sit on the back with the feed. It felt good when the wind blew in my hair.

Uncle Hubert was also a barber and had a big barber chair in the store where people sat to get a haircut. Sometimes he would let me sit in the big black chair and then he would make his foot go up and down and the chair would go up high. Uncle Hubert was a short man, so it made me feel tall.

Uncle Hubert and his brother Lester had a big carpenter shop where they made boats, and axe handles, and wheels. Sometimes the saw would make such a racket, like "Bzzzzzzzz", so that I couldn't hear anybody talking. There were always big piles of curly shavings on the floor and it was such fun to play with them. They had a wonderful smell, like something sweet. I would hold them up to Lester's head and say, "Now you look like me!" I would pretend he had ringlets too.

I loved it when Uncle Hubert played his violin, especially when he would play fast fiddle tunes and tap dance at the same time. He kept the violin in the store because Aunt Thelma didn't like the "noise" in the house. He told me he used to play his violin for silent movies.

Aunt Thelma was very talented too. She played the piano and I sat outside on the steps listening to the music. I especially loved it when she played "Nola" and "Stars are the Windows of Heaven." I could have sat there forever.

She made things with her sewing machine and would make beautiful stuffed animals like rabbits, and cats for the church to sell. I wanted to hug them all but I wasn't allowed to play with them in case I got them dirty. Aunt Thelma was very clean and didn't like it when we made a mess. I wished that she would make some animals just for me, but she never did.

All the people in St. Bernard were Catholic and the priest said that girls were not allowed to wear shorts, ever! We were not allowed to eat meat on Fridays either. Years later I attended a wiener roast on a Friday and thought for sure I would go to hell.

I went to church every Sunday with Uncle Hubert. Aunt Thelma never went—she said she had too much to do.

When we went into the church, people put their hand in a big bowl of water and then touched their foreheads, and their chest, and their shoulders. I had already washed before I came to church so didn't think I needed to do it again.

The priest used words that I didn't understand, like "Dominus Vobiscum" and "Et cum spiritu tuo". I wondered if this was a different kind of French or why the priest just didn't speak English. We had to kneel, then stand up, then kneel again, then stand up again. I just watched everybody else and did what they did. Sometimes people hit themselves in the chest and said "Kyrie eleison", whatever that meant. People lined up to go to the front and then they stuck their tongues out. I didn't think that was very nice.

I made my first communion in the big St. Bernard's church and was dressed in white with a veil. I told Uncle Hubert that I felt like an angel.

When I was very young, on the morning of December 24, 1947, I was put on a bus to visit with my mother in Halifax. It was Christmas Eve, and I was worried that Santa Claus wouldn't know where I was, but Uncle Hubert said, "Don't worry Laura, he'll find you." Before I left Aunt Thelma told me, "Get in there and use the bathroom"—and so I did. The buses didn't have toilets in those days. All was well for a while but then the winter cold made me want to pee again. Light snow had started to fall and by the time the bus left, there were big heaps of it. The Acadian Lines bus left on time with all seats full and with about five to eight people standing. My bladder was bursting and there was nowhere to go. I kept wondering how long before we arrived in Halifax. I kept looking out the window for a place that I thought the bus driver might stop for me. As soon as I saw a place and got up the nerve to ask the bus driver to stop, we had passed by those bushes. What was a little girl to do? I kept asking the person next to me, "What time is it please?" and "How much further to Halifax?" I was reaching the point where I didn't think I could stand and walk without wetting my pants so when the bus finally stopped in the halfway point, Middleton, for a break, I was afraid to move. And besides, what if the bus left me there? I had almost got up the courage when people began to file back onto the bus. Too late! I would have to wait, but I couldn't do it. I was in agony. I stared out the window and counted trees, counted houses, counted anything that moved. It was cold but I was sweating. Finally, as lady-like as I could, I stood up, moved my wool coat from underneath me, and sat down again. My bladder began to empty. The blue velour seat was becoming warm and so was I. When we arrived in Halifax I waited for everyone else to get off of the bus and then, as I rose, I leaned back to brush my hand across the seat to smooth it before I left. I often wondered who took my seat on the next trip.

One day my Aunt Thelma just decided that she didn't want to keep both my sister and me, and said, "One of you has to go." I was chosen to leave and my Uncle Hubert was crying and saying that I was his "buddy". I was sad. I was scared. I hugged my teddy bear close, and told him, "Don't be afraid. Maybe this will just be like a vacation."

I told myself that it must be because my little sister was cuter and that because I had polio and a lame leg I must be too much trouble. Maybe I had made too much mess, or used more than "one sheet of toilet paper for pee" or more than "two sheets for poop" like Aunt Thelma told me to. I guess I did sometimes, so it was my fault.

I was taken to live with my father's mother, Grammy Mabel, in a place called Centreville, a little village near the water on Digby Neck. Grammy Mabel had twelve children so I guess she didn't mind having one more. I would try hard to be good so they wouldn't want me to leave again.

Centreville is named for its location, halfway between Digby and Petit Passage. The area became Centreville in 1875. The main industry in Centreville is hand-lining and lobster fishing.

Grampy Ben was a fisherman and he always smelled like fish. I liked him so I didn't care what he smelled like. He used to tease Grammy Mabel about being so fat. "Sometimes I have to grease her and put my foot in her bum to get her through the door," he said. She heard him but she always laughed. She *was* fat, but I didn't dare laugh.

Their kitchen had a door in the floor and I had never seen one before. If you were strong enough, you could pull it up; but I couldn't. I watched Grammy as she grabbed the big iron ring and pulled it up to reveal a dark place. It looked scary to me and I suspected that the boogieman Mom used to warn me about lived down there. Grammy would walk down those steps and return with some vegetables and apples for our supper. Then she would close the floor door. I wouldn't have tried to open it no matter how much I wanted apples.

I tried hard to be good but maybe I wasn't good enough because soon they sent me to live with my father's sister, Agnes Tidd, who lived close by in Sandy Cove.

The Indians called it "Noogoomkegawaachk"—a small sandy cove. Fishing is the main industry here and on St. Mary's side a wharf is port to many types of fishing vessels such as draggers, scallop draggers and lobster boats.

Aunt Agnes and Uncle Angus had two children who were about my age, so I had someone to play with. Uncle Angus was a fisherman like my Grampy, but he didn't smell as good as he did. I was so happy to discover that there was a piano in their house and sometimes I was allowed to try and play a song on it. If only I could play one of those songs that Grammy Lil used to sing to me. But when I thought about her singing, it made me sad. I missed her so much I wanted to cry. But I would try not to.

I didn't live in Sandy Cove for very long. My mother came one day and told me I had to go with her. "But I don't want to," I told her. She grabbed my hand and pulled me out to the car anyway. She moved me to a place called Fall River with her sister Margaret Chalmers. I thought, "*Why doesn't anybody like me?*" I had been as good as I could be. "*What's wrong with me?*"

My Uncle Hubert had a sister Mattie who was an older lady and she and her husband Norman Doucette had no children. Uncle Hubert had spoken to Mattie and Norman about me living with them and they had agreed. It was in the same village as my little sister lived, about a mile away.

I arrived with my little suitcase and Mattie gave me a big hug. She wasn't much bigger than I was, it seemed. Their house didn't have a toilet inside, so I discovered I had to go to the outhouse at the back of the house. There were catalogues instead of toilet paper and Mattie told me what to do. "Tear out a page and crumple it up in your fist and roll it around to make it nice and soft." There were two holes cut in a big board and I decided to use the smaller one so I wouldn't fall in. The flies seemed to love that place better than I did but I loved looking at all the old pictures on the wall. There was no place to wash my hands until I went back into the house and I had to push the pump handle up and down to get some water. It made a "swish, swish" sound and the water would come out. At night when it was too dark to go to the outhouse, I had to use a pot that slid under my bed. I had to move the pot carefully so nothing would spill out; sometimes it did but I would find something to wipe it up so nobody would see it. I was tempted to use the sleeve of my nightgown but I never did; well, maybe once! Carrying that pot down the stairs without spilling it was a tricky business, but it had to be done. It wasn't my favourite job for sure.

In the evenings, Mattie would sit in a little rocking chair and rock back and forth; Norman would lie on the couch in the kitchen and listen to the radio. His big Popeye ashtray sat on a table beside him. I loved that Popeye figure and made believe he was my friend. Sometimes a noise would come from somewhere underneath Mattie's chair, like *Pfffft!* I knew she was passing gas; I wasn't allowed to call it the other word.

I started school in the little two-room school in St. Bernard. It was heated by a wood stove and the older kids had to bring in the firewood to make the fire and keep it going. In the morning it was really cold until the fire started to burn well. I loved the smell of wood burning. Sometimes it got too hot if the boys over-stuffed the stove and I would sweat. Our toilets were outdoors and we had to put our hand up and say, "Please may I leave the room?" The teacher would sometimes say "No" because some kids would only do this for an excuse to go outside. I never did. When I put my hand up, I was serious.

The lower grades were on the main floor and the higher grades were on the upstairs floor. My teacher was a lady named Rosie and I loved her dearly because she was so kind. I enjoyed visiting her home whenever I could. One day she said that she "knew that I would amount to something." Her words carried me through and I thought of them many times. It felt good that someone thought I was smart.

Living with Mattie and Norman was the first time I ever felt like I had a home. Mattie and I picked crates of blueberries to sell every week, and she made lots of delicious pies, cookies, and bread. Meals there were usually boiled potatoes and dried fish, the kind that you didn't have to cook. It was dry and salty and had lots of bones, but it tasted yummy. On Sundays we always had a roasted chicken.

We didn't have running water or an indoor toilet but they didn't seem like hardships. I remember dipping hot water out of the side of the stove to wash, standing beside the stove. Once a week, Mattie would fill a big old galvanized tub with warm water so I could get in and have a bath.

Norman trudged off to work every day with his lunch pail and I could hardly wait for him to come home again. I would hurry as fast as I could down the dirt road to meet him. Sometimes I would fall, but he would run and pick me up and dust me off, with the words, "Pauvre enfant." Norman always spoke French to me. I knew it meant "Poor child".

We were Catholic so went to church faithfully every Sunday. Evenings we had to get down on our knees and hold something that looked like a big necklace. They said it was called a rosary and the little balls were called beads. Then we would say prayers like "Je vous salut, Marie"—that meant "Hail Mary" in English"—and "Notre Pere qui es aux cieux"—which meant "Our Father, who art in Heaven". After saying the rosary I could have a gingersnap, so it had been worth it.

Confession and communion were regular affairs. I had so few sins to confess that sometimes I had to think hard to have something to tell the priest. Usually it was "I forgot my morning or my evening prayers".

One time Mattie caught me peeking up the leg of a little fellow's short pants. I was immediately marched off to confession. It seemed I had done a terrible thing and "shame on me." I was just curious and after all I hadn't even seen anything so I didn't know what they were so mad about.

Mattie, Norman and I used to go to church for what they called "Vespers" in the evenings sometimes. One day I had been out playing with a friend and I was too late getting home so they went without me. I ran to the church and quickly sat in a back pew just before the Vespers started. All was well until I saw them start to pass the collection basket. I didn't have any money, and what was I going to do? I was sure it was a sin not to put money in the collection and I had to do something. Just before they got to me, I leaned over to the man sitting beside me and said, "Can I borrow a nickel please?" Phew! Just in time, I dropped in my nickel!

Then one day my mother appeared in St. Bernard and wanted me to walk over to Aunt Thelma's, which was about a mile away. It didn't seem to matter to her that I walked with a limp and each step hurt; but I was used to that anyway. I remember that it was pouring rain, so Mattie dressed me in a rain hat and long raincoat a few times too big for me. When my mother saw my appearance she went into a fit and decided on the spot that I was not staying with "those people". She took me to live with her sister Margaret that day, without even letting Mattie and Norman know. It must have broken their hearts like it did mine.

Aunt Margaret was a widow now, and she had moved from Fall River to live in the middle of nowhere, in the woods, in a place called Morganville. I would have to travel to my new school in a taxi as there weren't any schools in Morganville. The houses were far apart but we had one close neighbour, Murray. He lived alone and used to show me how to use a whip. He would throw his arm high in the air, and then throw it forward with a "Whoosh"; the whip would make a loud sound like *Snap! Snap!* I didn't want to go too close. Sometimes he would invite me into his house, but I didn't go very often. I told him his house was "dark and smelly, and I don't think you're a very good housekeeper."

My mother and her sister Thelma fought constantly so it wasn't long before my sister Carmen came to live with me at Aunt Margaret's. Now we both traveled to school by taxi.

There were times living in Morganville that Carmen and I had a great time, mostly playing together outdoors and visiting an older couple, Polly and Leo. He was in a wheelchair but managed somehow to make us stilts to entertain us. It made me feel awfully tall and sometimes I fell off them, but I wanted to get right back up again. Carmen could walk on the stilts a lot better and faster than I could.

I was ten years old when my mother came to visit us in Morganville. She told me I was going to Halifax to live with her and her new husband Edward.

"You have to call him Daddy," Mom said.

"But he isn't my daddy." I didn't want to.

"He is now, and you will do what I say." She sounded mad and I knew better than to sass her.

Carmen would return to Aunt Thelma's. She and I would both be going to different schools again. I would miss my little sister, but was getting used to the idea of moving.

We arrived in Halifax and I had never seen so many houses and stores! Mom told me it was a city and lots of people lived here. "You're not going to be a country hick here," she said. I didn't know what a "country hick" was, but I would try not to be one.

Edward had three daughters, Marlene, Shirley, and Linda Lou. They were all older than I was. It was the first time I had ever seen a glass eye and was told how Linda Lou had accidentally stuck a can opener in her eye and that it had to be removed. I thought how that must have hurt!

I would watch Linda Lou take her glass eye out and then put it in a dish to soak in water. It looked like my doll's eyes. Once Linda Lou pulled her eyelid up so I could see what was in there. It looked all pink. "So that's what's behind my eye!" I wondered if my eye could come out too, but didn't dare try in case I couldn't get it back in.

Shirley and I became good friends. Marlene was older and more interested in boys, as was Linda Lou. Linda Lou liked to travel on the buses at night using a bus pass. One time she got one for me too and took me along. It was kind of fun until she got off the bus with some boys, and I had to go with her. One of the boys tried to kiss me and I was scared, but Linda Lou was busy somewhere else. I pushed the boy away, and he let me go. I ran as fast as I could hollering, "Linda Lou, Linda Lou!" I guess she didn't hear me. I didn't know what to do so just kept running.

Once I was asked to do an errand. I was to go to the bakery and buy some frosted cupcakes for a neighbour. They looked delicious and I hoped they would give me one. The baker tied a string around the box to make it easier for me to carry. It was a rainy day and muddy and maybe that's why I slipped and fell. The string around the box broke and the cupcakes tumbled onto the wet gravel. What now? I did the only thing I could think of. I picked up the cupcakes, and one by one I used my finger to smooth out the frosting, gravel and all. I delivered the cupcakes and ran—I didn't want a cupcake now. Did I make a dentist rich that day? I'll never know. They never asked me to go to the store again.

It wasn't long before I learned to fear my stepfather Edward. He was a taxi driver and often arrived home with a trunk load of stolen goods and alcohol. I heard that he "boot-legged" but I didn't know what that meant. Maybe he sold boots?

Edward was a fat man with a reddish face, and not much hair on his head. He usually smelled like he had been drinking alcohol. He had a habit of coming up behind his daughters and wrapping his arms and hands around their breasts, and decided he would include me. I was only eleven years old. It was disgusting and it was scary. He sometimes spun me around and tried to plant a wet slobbering kiss on my lips. I hated it, but Mom didn't seem to object. Maybe she didn't want another beating.

I witnessed Edward hitting Mom many times, and sometimes after the beating she and I would move to another place. She would always go back to live with Edward after a couple of days. One move found us in a small upstairs apartment in downtown Halifax. Mom worked at the Arcade Ladies Shop close by.

I enjoyed going to CYO, a Catholic Youth Organization located in another part of the city, and at twelve years old I traveled alone on a bus at night. It was dark as I stood waiting for the bus, and it was frightening being alone. Once I arrived on Barrington Street, I had to walk several blocks back to our apartment. I was scared so walked as fast as I could.

One night as I entered our apartment building I heard shouting coming from our place. Edward had discovered where we were living. I opened the door and saw him lying on our bed in the bed-sitting room. His face was bright red, and he was shouting, "You bitch! You rotten bitch!" He kept hitting the wall with his fist and punched a hole in it the size of a grapefruit. I wanted to run, but I couldn't leave Mom alone with him. As I entered, I walked on pieces of glass—they were all over the floor. Mom was drunk and staggering, and just tilted her chin in the air as she so often did. Edward got up off of the bed when he saw me and swung his fist at my mother.

"Stop!" I screamed at him.

"Don't you holler at me again!" he yelled at me. "My daughters never did and you're not going to. If you yell at me again, I'll throw you through that window!"

The window was open and we were on the third floor, but that thought didn't stop me from screaming as he struck her once more: "No! Stop hitting her!"

Too late, his 250 lb. body was coming for me. The good Lord had to be with me that night as I ducked under his arm and was able to escape into the hallway. Neighbours had gathered. I have no more memory of anything else that happened that night except that I had an earache for quite a while afterwards.

In Halifax I attended St. Joseph's School for grades 6, 7, and 8 and was taught by the Sisters of Charity. We wore navy blue uniforms, bulky blue bloomers and a scarf tie colour-coded according to our grade. We had to line up outdoors and a bell sounded to announce the beginning of the school day. The Victrola record player in the hallway played a march as we entered the school and marched up the stairs in single file, directly to our classroom. Our days began with prayer. Every first Friday of the month we were led to church for confession, to be sure all of our sins were forgiven before receiving communion at Sunday mass. We had better get through Saturday sin-free. We had been told, "If you die with any sins on your soul before you confess them to the priest, you aren't going to heaven."

Attending a Catholic school meant strict discipline. If you dropped something or made a noise, you were expected to say, "I'm sorry." The nuns were dressed in their long black habits and I often wondered how they starched those pure white collars and headdresses. They had names like Sister John Hugh, and Sister Joseph William, which seemed strange for women. They were scary and it was worth your life to anger them.

St. Joseph's School was for girls only and the Alexander MacKay School for boys was across the street. I remember being caught looking through the window across the street at the boys and was called to the Principal's office with a few other girls. "You have sinned!" she said.

One morning the nuns gave us tickets to sell and said, "Be sure to sell them all." I went home for lunch and didn't go back to school until mid-afternoon, but my tickets were all sold. It didn't occur to me that the nun meant I should sell them in my own time. I think the teacher should have said what she meant.

My mother, for reasons best known to herself, decided that we would move to Saint-Eustache, Quebec, with her sister Isabel Parker. It was my first airplane ride and I threw up. I felt better when the stewardess gave me some candy.

Aunt Isabel worked in a ladies dress shop in Montreal and Uncle Donald was an artist. I wanted to watch him draw and told him, "I won't bother you, Uncle Donald." I didn't bother him, but sometimes he bothered me when he wanted me to sit on his lap. There was something bumpy and hard there and I didn't like it.

We were there for only two weeks before we returned to Halifax and Edward. The nun teacher at St. Joseph's School seemed angry at me for disrupting her class by coming back. "Sit down in your seat!" "Pay attention!" "Don't be so slow!"

My mother's sister "Aunt Madelyn" and her husband, "Uncle Mike" lived in Halifax and had three little boys who I enjoyed playing with. Sometimes Mom and I would visit when Aunt Madelyn was home, but mostly when her husband Uncle Mike was there alone. Mom and Uncle Mike would both be drinking, and sometimes they would hug each other. The rooms didn't have doors, just long curtains in the doorways, so it was easy to see and hear what was going on in the bedroom. I tried not to look but I was wondering what the noise was all about and peeked in. Mom and Uncle Mike were on the bed. I didn't think Aunt Madelyn would be happy about that. I sure wasn't going to tell her.

One day Mom and I went to Aunt Madelyn's place. Aunt Isabel had arrived from Quebec and was visiting with her. I was happy to see her again and told her so. I was playing with the other kids outside in the snow when I heard a lot of hollering from inside the house. I was used to hearing a lot of hollering but the hollering was getting louder and it sounded to me like they were fighting. I wondered if Aunt Madelyn had discovered that Mom and Uncle Mike had been hugging and kissing and now she was mad at her. Then the hollering stopped and I heard people crying. Soon I heard a loud siren; it kept getting louder and louder and then a big ambulance appeared. It stopped outside Aunt Madelyn's place and some people with white shirts and dark pants ran in. I went inside to see what was happening. Aunt Madelyn was lying on the floor and there was blood coming from her head. Her eyes were wide open but she wasn't crying. Everybody was talking at once so I couldn't understand what was going on. Nobody would tell me what had happened. They just said, "Never mind, you don't need to know." I saw them put Aunt Madelyn on a big stretcher and carry her outside. Then they put her into the back of the ambulance and closed the door. The next day I heard them say that Aunt Madelyn had hit her head on a radiator and had died. She was only 36 years old. Now her three little boys wouldn't have a mommy—but at least they had a daddy.

Years later I located her death certificate. It showed the cause of her death as "Subarachnoid Hemorrhage" and it also said that she "died suddenly at home without medical care". There had been an autopsy. I read further information which said "a traumatic blow to the head can cause subarachnoid hemorrhage" and that "an autopsy may not be able to answer the question of causation".

Had Aunt Madelyn really "fallen" or had she been pushed during the fighting I had heard? The only ones who knew the answer to that question were Mom and Aunt Isabel. I would never know!

At thirteen years of age, I started Grade 9; the first year that St. Patrick's School was built in Halifax. Boys and girls were in the same classes, and I was glad I no longer had to wear a blue tunic and bulky bloomers. I was enjoying school and was voted class president. I didn't know what a president was supposed to do, but I felt important anyway.

My mother had left Edward once more, and we had moved into a small apartment in Halifax where we shared the same bed. At that time Barrington Street was considered the ghetto of the city and I was embarrassed to tell anyone where I lived. Mom was always drinking but somehow managed to keep her job with the Arcade Ladies Shop. Sometimes I would go there to help out and was allowed to try to sell clothing. Most of the time I was kept busy folding clothes and addressing envelopes. I was given a pay envelope with a few dollars for my hard work and it was nice to have money of my own for a change.

Mom would frequently go out for entertainment and one night I awoke to another body in the bed. It was a man, and I bolted and ran. I didn't know where I was going, but I was getting out of there! As I was trying to get dressed, my mother caught me and ripped the blouse off of my back. I started to cry but with a hard slap across my face, Mom made sure I stopped. The strange man was awake now and said that he thought he should leave. I thought he should leave too, but kept quiet. Mom smiled at him sweetly as she walked him to the door and kissed him good-bye. Once she had closed the door, she glared at me angrily and just stuck her chin in the air. Without another word, she went back to bed. It was in the wee hours of the morning and I was tired and confused. I didn't want to get back in *that* bed. I finally lay down on the sofa, covered myself with my coat and fell asleep. When I awoke my mother had already left for work. I was glad I didn't have to see her or talk to her that morning. Still tired and sleepy, somehow I managed to get ready for school.

I was not as alert as I should have been to write my school exams that day.

Chapter Two

Bear River

One day my Aunt Margaret arrived to take us to live in her house in Bear River. She wanted Mom to move there to care for my grandmother Lil and Mr. Davidson, the elderly gentleman who had agreed to leave his house to her if she would care for him until he died. He was now in his nineties and people had been taking advantage of him by taking things from his home. There were still many beautiful pieces of furniture like grape-back settees, huge gold-framed mirrors, and wonderful old sets of dishes. My Aunt Margaret would inherit all of this because my mother was going to look after Mr. Davidson. Aunt Margaret could continue to work as a nurse.

When we arrived in Bear River I noticed a big sign that read: "Bear River, the Switzerland of Nova Scotia." I had read about Switzerland and knew only that it had many high hills; maybe that's what the sign meant as we did drive up and down some really steep hills on the way to Aunt Margaret's. When we drove through town, we crossed a little bridge and I could see that the stores and many of the houses seemed to be sitting on tall wooden stilts on the riverbanks. They reminded me of the stilts Leo used to make for Carmen and me when we lived in Morganville. But these were a whole lot bigger.

When we arrived at Aunt Margaret's house Grammy Lil met us at the door. I was so happy to see her that I just couldn't let go of her hand and clung to her like glue. The house seemed awfully large compared to where I had lived before. It was located on the main street of Bear River. It had three entrances; one led into the dining room, one into a big hallway where you could see a wide, tall staircase, and the other door entered into the back porch and kitchen. On the main floor there was a kitchen and pantry, dining room, living room and large bedroom. There was a fireplace in each room except for the kitchen where there was a wood stove. As I said before, I loved the smell of wood burning. A set of stairs led from the kitchen to the upstairs where there were five bedrooms and a bathroom. Another stairway led downstairs again. Mom was always in the kitchen smoking cigarettes when we came downstairs in the morning.

Notices began appearing in the *Digby Courier* newspaper. They read, "Thank you to Margaret Chalmers and Lillian Derline for doing for her what she couldn't do for herself." It was Edward placing ads in the local newspaper. He was referring to my aunt and grandmother who had helped Mom to move out of the city. The ads continued for some time, and each one was a little scarier than the last if you knew what he was hinting at.

Then one day just before Christmas, a man arrived at the door and said, "I was asked to deliver four Christmas trees five feet high." It didn't make sense until I overheard Mom and Aunt Margaret talking about Edward: "He is going to tie each of us to a tree and set fire to it!" Where did that come from? Had he told them that? I was scared to death and looked over my shoulder everywhere I went. I imagined Edward jumping out of nowhere to grab me.

Christmas at our house was a time to trim the tree, one icicle at a time, hung straight, and hung evenly. It was a thing of beauty—something to look at, not enjoy. Presents were placed under the tree, all in a row, in a straight row, not to be moved until Christmas morning.

As the presents were opened, each one had to be placed back under the tree in its box for display, in a row, in a straight row, not to be moved until company came. Then it was show and tell time. "I got this from so and so", and then folded carefully and put back in the box, carefully, in a row, in a straight row, not to be moved until company came again.

Then late one night, after we had all gone to bed, the doorbell rang. I was upstairs in my bed and heard loud voices downstairs. It sounded like Edward and my heart almost stopped beating. Every muscle in my body tensed as I strained to listen. It *was* Edward and I knew that could only mean trouble. The voices were getting louder and louder and I could tell that Mom and Edward were fighting. I didn't dare move. Then I heard what sounded like a knife being sharpened on a stone, and the sound was getting louder. Back and forth, back and forth it continued, "Whish, slap, whish, slap", and then his loud laughter. It sent shivers up my spine.

I realized I couldn't hear Mom anymore and it wasn't like her to be so quiet. My bedroom was beside the stairway leading to the kitchen and I could tell that Edward was now standing at the bottom of the kitchen stairs. Horrified, I tensed into a fetal position and waited for his footsteps. I said a prayer and asked God to please help me. The "Whish, Slap" noise stopped and Mom was talking quietly now. I supposed she had somehow pacified Edward, perhaps by giving him a drink. Within a very short time I heard them talking outside; then I heard a car start. I assumed he had left and I crept down to Grammy Lil's bedroom. She had been as frightened as I was and we hugged tightly. She had a bad heart and I worried about her. When we went out to the kitchen, Mom was sitting at the table drinking. Her face was red and puffy and she had some scratches on her arms. All she said was, "Go back to bed! He's gone!" Edward never came back to Bear River. I heard much later that he had been admitted to a Mental Hospital.

I attended Oakdene School in Bear River and managed to tie for first place at the end of the year. I was now going into Grade 10. Oakdene School only taught up to Grade 9, so the next year I traveled by bus into Digby, to Digby Regional High School.

The trip took about a half hour and on the way to school we had to pass a piggery. In the summers, the smell from the pigs was foul and kids would hold their noses and say P-U. It was an awful smell, and you had to hold your breath until the bus passed. Even if the windows of the bus were not open—you couldn't get away from the smell.

Kids knew that I could speak French and so they often asked me to translate their French assignments on the drive to and from school. My nickname became "Frenchy".

I was sitting on the bus on the way home when one of the boys was on the way to his seat. As he walked by, he reached out and grabbed my breast and grinned, and then sat down opposite me. I was startled, but sat staring straight ahead. I watched him out of the corner of my eye and saw my opportunity to take the grin off his face. My hand swung back and then forward to land right on his cheek where I had aimed: "Whoosh, smack!" His face was redder than mine now, and he wasn't grinning anymore.

Studying did not come easy for me but I was always able to memorize enough to pass exams and even get good marks. I had everybody fooled. They thought I was smart, but I knew better. I had been told many times by my mother, "You're so stupid." I assumed that the polio had affected my brain.

Yet somehow my ability to memorize carried me through even though I often didn't understand a thing. I had such a great ability to memorize that when in exams, I could recall the answer to questions by picturing the page and even the page number. It was like my mind had taken a picture of the pages, and when I wanted to, I could look at them in detail. I would have to change a few words or else the teachers would think I had somehow copied.

My mother was a very pretty lady with a petite figure, never weighing more than 100 pounds. She cooked but didn't eat, yet she piled our plates full to the outer edge, and she said we had better eat it all. She never sat at the table with us for meals, and come to think of it, I hardly ever saw her eat anything except a bowl of cereal at night.

She scared the daylights out of me and so I stayed out of her way as best I could. My grandmother tried to do the same as she tiptoed to the kitchen in her housedress for her breakfast—a cup of tea with her saccharin tablet, half a grapefruit and maybe cereal. She huddled in the kitchen nook quietly as my mother tore about. "Jesus Christ Mama, what do you think this is, a God-dammed hotel?" Many times Grammy Lil escaped to the safety of her bedroom in tears, with me following. We were a great comfort to each other.

Our best times were when Mom went out. Then our world came alive with Grammy Lil playing the piano and me singing and playing the spoons. Her fingers seemed to dance over the piano keys like magic. I loved the songs she played, and learned all the words to "Wish Me Luck as You Wave Me Goodbye" by Gracie Fields, "Down By the Old Mill Stream", "Isle of Capri", and "Oh 'Dem Golden Slippers".

Grammy Lil played the pump organ in the only Catholic Church on 'Indian Hill'. The church was on the 'Reservation' high up on a hill and a drive over dirt roads. Most of the congregation consisted of native Micmac but they called them Indians. People seemed to appear out of nowhere as they came out of the trees and bushes from their homes. They looked different to me. Their skin was darker than mine and their hair was jet black and straight. My favourite Micmac lady was Betty Harlow. She was a big and cheerful lady and used to call my Grammy Lil "Sweetheart", and she called me "Honey". Betty was all dressed up with her blue satin high heels and work socks for Sunday church. Many of the older people had wrinkles—wrinkles that looked like withered apples. The choir consisted of whoever felt like singing that day, so mostly songs were sung off-key. Sometimes I had to get down on the floor and pump the organ pedals with my hands; Grammy Lil found it tiring to do it with her feet, I guess because there was a hole in the bellows. Some of the men would get up and go outside when the collection plate was passed, and enter again to take their seats after that was over. Maybe they didn't have any money and were embarrassed to stay, or maybe they wanted to save their money for alcohol.

There was a huge statue of the Virgin Mary at the back of the church. One of her feet was broken off, so I got some plaster and built her a new one. I think she probably blessed me that day. I knew what it was like to have one foot different from the other one.

There was an old pump organ in our outside building and I began to spend time there, even in the freezing cold winter. I wanted to learn to play the organ like my grandmother. Armed with only a couple of old music books and a little knowledge about music notes I had learned in school, I began to play "Annie Laurie" and a few hymns. I wanted to take music lessons. Piano lessons were $1.00 and each week I walked to my one-hour lessons. Problems with my right hand co-ordination made it difficult to strike the proper chords on the piano but I was determined to learn.

Practicing at home became impossible. Each time I tried, my mother would slam the door to the dining room where the piano was located.

I finally gave up rather than incur Mom's further wrath, and turned my attention to greater things like helping to clean the house. Each Saturday morning I got up and busied myself with whatever needed to be done. Sleeping in was not an option. With six bedrooms, a living room, dining room, kitchen, pantry, porches, and bathroom, there was a lot of cleaning to be done. Mom would holler, "Everything has to be dusted and polished!" The silverware was the hardest.

There were two very special "characters" who lived in Bear River—"Banjo" Jordan and "Walli" Parker.

"Banjo" was born in Bear River, and had fourteen brothers and sisters; they were the only black family in town. His ancestors came to Nova Scotia as Black Loyalists and received large land grants in the Bear River area. At five feet, one inch tall, "Banjo" bustled around town, greeting everyone. We had only one STOP sign in the town, and every Saturday evening the stores remained open. "Banjo" would stand beside the stop sign and direct traffic. He was always dressed sharply in bright red slacks, a white shirt and tie, and a top hat. He'd always wink at the ladies; they said he was a "ladies' man".

"Banjo" used to look after the outdoor skating rink behind the Bear River Fire Hall. He made sure the ice was smooth as silk, and used to freeze pictures of the Queen and Royalty in the ice surface. It was a sight to behold. For many years he faithfully ran the outdoor skating rink and he taught many of the young people how to skate. I used to try but with my two feet being different sizes and with skates of only one size, my left foot was cramped and frequently got frozen. It was painful when I took off my skate. I used to hold my foot and try to grin and bear the pain. It helped that "Banjo" kept a warm fire burning in the little shed beside the rink.

One of the things Mom was great at was skating. She used to glide across the ice like she was flying. I often wished I could skate like she did, but I could hardly stand on skates, let alone glide. It was there that she met "Walli".

"Walli" Parker was Bear River's first hippie. He always dressed in raggedy clothes and I remember him having a big safety pin in the front of his pants where the zipper had been. He had once been a Bank Manager but he had long since chosen a different lifestyle. He lived with his Uncle Clement in an old house on a hill. Walli was also a wonderful skater so before too long he and Mom were skating together. Mom began to invite him for meals at our house. One evening she wanted to go dancing and managed to outfit Walli with a sports coat and slacks. He sure looked dapper! He was a kind and gentle soul. Sometimes he would catch me crying and I would feel better after he talked to me.

Mr. Davidson and my grandmother would sit and watch TV in the evening and Grammy Lil loved the wrestling matches. She would sit on a footstool close to the TV and yell, "Come on! Watch out!" Of course, she also liked to watch "Lawrence Welk" because of the old songs they sang; and so did I.

We also watched "Bishop Sheen" on TV. I heard a story about how once Bishop Sheen arrived at an airport and there were reporters there. One said to him, "I suppose the first place you will want to visit will be the tavern?" Bishop Sheen said, "Oh, is there a tavern in the town?" The next day the newspaper headlines read, "FIRST QUESTION BISHOP SHEEN ASKS, 'Is there a tavern in the town?'"

Mr. Davidson was growing old and became ill so now he stayed in bed most of the time. One night I heard him talking and went in to see if anything was wrong. He said he could see big golden lights and angels and asked me if I could see them too. I said I did to make him feel better. Not too long after that Mr. Davidson died.

My Aunt Margaret who now owned the house we all lived in kept her own little apartment in the nurse's residence but came home for the weekends. When she was home her preference was for brandy rather than beer like my mother drank. Slurred speech was the norm in our household, except for my dear Grammy Lil who never had a drink in her life.

There were frequent arguments between Mom and Aunt Margaret, usually about money and something my mother wanted her to buy. One of her wants was a large Myna bird that was supposed to talk. She named him Joe. Every day we were told to practice with him, "My name is Joe, my name is Joe." And he would reply "Arrrrrrk!" He was huge and looked like a crow with his big black feathers. Maybe he *was* a crow. He sat on a perch in a cage big enough to hold an elephant—well, almost! He smelled like rotten eggs. His cage was in the dining room, of all places.

All he ever said was "Arrrrrrk" and finally Mom wanted to return him from whence he came. Lucky for him he left, or we might have ended up eating Myna bird stew.

Sunday mornings I was off to church with Grammy Lil. Sunday afternoons usually meant a visit from Aunt Thelma and Uncle Hubert who brought my sister Carmen with them. Fights between Aunt Thelma and Mom were inevitable. Whenever the hollering started, Grammy Lil would head for her bedroom, and say, "Come with me." It wasn't pleasant to be around the arguments and usually nasty things were said. I couldn't decide who was the nastiest, Mom or Aunt Thelma. Uncle Hubert would sneak outdoors so he wouldn't get involved. I knew he was sneaking a drink of whiskey but never told. Why they continued to visit was beyond my understanding.

I arrived home from church one Sunday and my mother in her drunken stupor was determined to go to Halifax. Not wanting her to go alone, I went with her and we boarded a bus. Within a few minutes, my mother was sick and vomiting. Not to anyone's disappointment we got off the bus in the middle of nowhere. Mom was staggering. Somehow I got a taxi for the return trip to Bear River and the driver was not impressed when she vomited in his car. We arrived back in Bear River to "Home, Sweet Home".

Grammy Lil would often say, "She's my own, and I love her, but my God she's cranky." She never swore, but did say "My God". Mom was not always nasty. She excelled when anyone was sick, and I wanted to be sick so she would be nice to me. Clean sheets, fluffed pillows, and meals in bed. I wanted to be sick forever. Sometimes I even pretended to be sick.

For some unknown reason, perhaps to make extra money, my mother decided she wanted to take in boarders. She worked hard cooking meals and cleaning and each day the dining room table was set. It was set perfectly; a fresh white linen tablecloth, more than one fork and knife and numerous spoons at each place setting, with a bread and butter plate and butter knife on each one. I learned to set a table properly and had better put the cream and sugar exactly where they were supposed to go.

Grace was never said at our table as God was not taken into consideration in any discussions. Religion was Catholic—if anyone asked.

Once Mom made a lemon pie with heaps of meringue for the old man across the street. It sat to cool in the pantry as I was reaching for the vinegar cruet—oops! The vinegar fell into the pie! There was not a chance that I was going to tell Mom what had happened so when she told me to deliver the pie, I did just that. She would never know.

A widower Thomas "Mac" MacGregor came to live with us as a boarder and he and Mom soon became very close. They seemed to get along famously. I had never seen her so attentive to anyone before. He got along well with my grandmother, and I liked him except for the times he would pick his nose. He did this continually and I could ignore it except for the times he was sitting at the dinner table. It made me sick to my stomach but Mom didn't seem to notice or if she did, she never mentioned it, so neither did I.

Grammy Lil loved to play cards and went to the weekly card games in our community. I wanted her to teach me to play Auction 45 so I could go with her. It was there that I noticed a young fellow with a red jacket who had a twinkle in his eye. It didn't occur to me that the twinkle was from the beer he was drinking. I started to look forward to the card games and seeing Clarence. When he returned to College we started to correspond. When he came home for visits we got together. It seemed that I had my first crush.

Grade 10 graduation meant a graduation dance and I felt like a princess dressed in a long gown. It was mauve with silver sparkles and it was borrowed from a friend of the family. I was only 14 years old and Clarence was my date. He was home from college. He took me parking, which was the usual "date" in our town. Kissing was my limit, mostly because of the fear the Catholic Church had instilled in me and the warnings from my mother to put me in a "home" if I got "into trouble". And besides, I thought if I "did anything" no one else would ever want me. That's what the Catholic Church had taught me and I firmly believed it. Clarence came for visits to the house and my mother reacted by pointing her finger in my face and saying, "If you ever come home pregnant, I'll put you in a home, little girl." Could you get pregnant from kissing?

I was so inexperienced and so naïve.

♣

Grade 11 and I was now fifteen years old. I was teased unmercifully about the hair on my upper lip—my mustache, as the boys called it. I had inherited the French gene which caused many of the French Acadian women to have facial hair. On a trip to the drugstore I discovered a hair remover called Neet and brought it home and proceeded to apply it. It burned like crazy and sometimes left redness where my mustache had been, but the hair was gone. Proud as punch, I thought, "Now they won't tease me." How wrong I was became clear when one of the boys called me over to their group and bent his head down to look at me. "Looks like you got a clean shave this morning," he grinned. I was humiliated. Boys were mean and insensitive.

I was asked out on a date by a fellow named Wendell Woolaver. Excited, I got all dressed up and waited for him to arrive to pick me up. I waited, and waited, and waited. He never did show up. It seems it was just a joke and he never intended to take me out. So many of the girls had boyfriends and partied but I was never included. I was sure it was because of my smaller leg and limp. No one wanted to date a girl like that when there were lots of pretty girls with "normal" legs.

"Nice leg—at least one of them is." I will never forget how I felt when a boy in a group of boys walking behind me made the comment. He will never know the effect he had on my life. Suddenly I realized people really did notice that one leg was smaller than the other one. This was a turning point for me and from that day on I never wanted to walk ahead of anyone again. I always tried to walk behind others so no one could see. I wanted to wear long skirts to hide my smaller leg. If they didn't see IT, they would think I was "normal", like everyone else.

"What size shoe do you take?" That question was always a little bit of an embarrassment to me as I had one foot size 5 AA and the other was probably a 7. I never knew for sure since I was made to wear one size for both feet, usually a size 6. Imagine having one shoe stuffed with Kleenex in the toe, and insoles, and the other shoe so tight that your toes had to bend in order to get it on. Every step was awkward and walking was far from enjoyable. As I became older I yearned to wear high heels like the other girls. Heels were stylish and so I persisted in trying to walk in them. My left foot could handle it but the right foot turned over with each step. I felt so feminine with high heels and looked great as long as I stood still.

For Physical Education everyone had to wear the same outfit, a short gym uniform. How could I hide now? The truth was out! Everyone would see. I was forced to be on display on the gym floor and there was nowhere to hide. Legs everywhere and often the thought ran through my mind, "Why couldn't I have had two legs the same? No matter what size they were as long as they matched." I was pretty but thought I would have traded it for an ugly face if only I had nice legs.

Grade 11 graduation found me without a date for the graduation dance. Clarence had said he would take me, but at the last minute he had changed his mind. He made up an excuse and arranged for his cousin Roy to take me. Little did I know that Clarence was seeing another girl, a Linda Lingley from Round Hill. She was a busty blonde. Roy picked me up for the dance and we went with a friend of mine, Pat Morine and her date, Marshall Darres.

We had a great time but when they wanted to go out in the car for the break, kissing was happening. I wouldn't let Roy come near me. "No, I am going out with Clarence." They knew he had another girlfriend but I didn't. Both Roy and Marshall tried their darndest to tell me the truth but I wasn't hearing it. It soon became clear when Clarence no longer came around nor called. I guessed that his other girlfriend was "giving in" and I wasn't "giving out."

After graduating from Grade 11, I attended St. Patrick's Business College where I took a Secretarial course. I never mentioned a word at home about having days off from school and went anyway. My teacher Sister Agnes Charles was surprised to see me typing away and I told her I just wanted to practice. I was finding it difficult to type because my right hand still lacked proper co-ordination from the polio.

During my time at St. Patrick's Business College, surrounded by Sisters of Charity, I wanted the peace they projected. Their black flowing gowns swished as they walked, and their huge white collars were so white I thought there had to be a word that meant whiter than white. Their headdress covered any hair and half of their forehead. I gave serious thought to becoming a nun. After all, I would always be able to hide my leg under the long gown.

I had wanted to be a nurse but both Mom and Aunt Margaret discouraged me by saying they knew I could never stand on my feet for as long as a nurse had to. There never was any discussion about going to University or what I might want to do for work. It seemed I would be destined to become a Secretary. After all, what else could someone who was lame do? I'd be lucky if anyone hired me.

One day Mr. Grant Reid, the Manager of the Royal Bank of Canada in Bear River visited the Business College. He knew I lived in Bear River and was interested in hiring me. Sister Agnes Charles recommended me, and so my first job meant that I would continue to live at home.

I was seventeen in February, 1959, and started work as a teller that April. My salary was $1,700 a year before taxes and I paid $35 every two weeks for room and board. I was not going to get rich and had very little money left over to spend. I received a letter from Carmen. She had enclosed a picture cut from a catalog. She wanted the record player and asked me to buy it for her. I was happy to.

Arriving at the bank for work, I was surprised not to see Mr. Reid there. He was such a hard worker, and a joy to work for. He never missed a day. When I left at the end of work the day before, he was still there and I asked if there was anything I could help him with. He declined my offer. That was the last time I ever saw Mr. Reid. They eventually found his suicide note in what was then known as the "Manager's can." He had driven his little car off of the end of the Digby wharf and drowned. He was survived by his wife and young son George. I often wondered if it would have changed anything if I had helped him a little more. There were only two of us working at the bank at this time, myself and Jim Wilkins. The washroom was in the basement. It was dark down there and Mr. Reid had kept his coveralls hanging on a line for times he would have to look through old boxes. Seeing those large coveralls hanging in the dark was spooky. There was no such thing as grief counseling but I might have benefited from it. I was haunted.

Eventually a new bank manager arrived, a Mr. Blair Hoskins. He was far different from Mr. Reid, and had a brusque and sarcastic manner. As tellers we had to balance our money daily. One day I was "out" a small amount of money and could not find where I had made a mistake. Mr. Hoskins insinuated that I might have taken it. I was upset with the insinuation since I had never taken anything in my life. When I told Mom my story she was at the bank the next day giving Mr. Hoskins a piece of her mind. That was more embarrassing and upsetting than the insinuation. The error was found later and it was not my fault after all, but I never liked Mr. Hoskins after his unjust accusation.

I had heard that "an old flame is easily rekindled" and so it was that on one of Clarence's trips home from Agriculture College, we got together again. It had been said by many that I was a very pretty girl—brown curly hair, green eyes, a tiny figure and "almost" perfect. I didn't blame Clarence for wanting to see me.

I still held on to my virginity but Clarence was pressuring me to "Put out, or get out." He told me how much it hurt him. Finally, in a well-planned scenario, I would get a bolt for my bedroom door, and at night he would climb up on the slanted roof to my bedroom and enter through an open window. Thinking back now, it was a stupid, stupid plan but a plan no less. It was late at night when everyone else had gone to bed; and hopefully asleep. Dressed in my nightgown, I sat waiting beside my open window watching for Clarence. He arrived and was quickly inside my room and into my bed with his clothes on. I was extremely nervous but there was no backing out now. He showed me a little circular foil package, and then opened it to reveal a rubber condom inside. Clarence said that he would "use" it to be sure that I didn't get pregnant. I had never seen one before and wondered how it worked; it didn't seem to come with instructions. But Clarence seemed to know what to do. He put the condom on and rolled it up. It looked like a rubber glove but with only one finger. As he lay on top of me he quickly entered. (As Captain Kirk said in Star Trek, "to boldly go where no man had gone before"!) He was getting increasingly excited and making noises that I was afraid someone might hear. It hurt, and I didn't feel any passion at all—I would have liked to, but I didn't. This was something I felt I *had* to do to keep Clarence from leaving me. I wanted it to be over quickly and before long it was. Clarence seemed contented and there he was, lighting a cigarette! I was anxious for him to leave. If anyone had smelled the smoke I suppose the worse they could accuse me of was sneaking cigarettes. The bolted door assured our privacy but how stupid could I get!

And so I had had my first sexual encounter. After this "episode" I prayed hard that I wouldn't become pregnant—and I didn't.

Chapter Three

For Better or Worse

In December 1959, Clarence gave me an engagement ring and asked me to marry him. Of course I said "Yes" without hesitation. What was there to think about? As I had heard from the Catholic Church many times, "If you have sex before you get married, no one else will ever want you." I was excited and couldn't wait to show my ring to everyone. Mom appeared shocked and reacted by saying, "You need my permission; you're not eighteen yet." I was only seventeen and could wait for a few months, but I knew now I would get married and live happily every after, just as the storybooks said. Best of all, I would no longer have to live in a house with my mother! I could hardly wait.

Clarence had previously attended college in Truro, but had managed to get into enough deviltry to be "kicked out" of his program. Now he would get serious about studying and applied to MacDonald College in Quebec. He would have a wife to support and would get his degree. Our plan was to move to Ste. Anne de Bellevue so he could attend college.

Our wedding date was set for August 15, 1960. The service was to be held in the little Catholic Church on Indian Hill in Bear River. Invitations were sent, a Hall was booked for the reception, and a wedding cake was to be made by a lady in the community. Grammy Lil was happy to be asked to play the organ. Clarence drove me to the city to look for my wedding gown. I had visions of white lace, sequins and pearls, with a long full flowing skirt. I wanted it to be perfect. Clarence couldn't understand why I just didn't buy the first gown I saw. "It was a wedding dress, wasn't it?" It was ironic that after looking for hours, I went back and decided on the very first gown I had tried on. Wedding colors were determined by the bridesmaid gowns I was able to borrow. They happened to be pink and yellow. Mom made the most adorable white dress for my flower girl. All was ready except for the flowers. A quick trip to our flower gardens in the backyard and the wedding bouquets were ready. I really hadn't wanted to carry gladioli and would have much preferred roses, but Mom made all the decisions and I didn't argue.

My father's brother "Uncle John" drove me to the church and on the way there he turned to me and said, "It's not too late to change your mind, you know." I wondered why he would say that but didn't ask him. I was sure it really *was* too late; all the wedding gifts had been received, all the guests were at the church, I was dressed in a beautiful white gown and Clarence was waiting. There was no turning back now! We arrived at the church and waited outside. The entrance was far too small for the wedding party and I was thankful it was a sunny day. Many of the local Indian folk had gathered to watch and wish me "Good Luck". I heard the organ begin to play the "Wedding March" and my stomach tightened into knots. Was it really too late to run? It should have been the happiest day of my life; I should want to run up the aisle but instead my feet acted like they were glued to the ground. Uncle John took my arm and moved me forward to follow the bridesmaids and flower girl. Everyone in the church was looking at me and smiling and I knew I was a beautiful bride. I could see Clarence waiting at the front—I was going to be his wife! The priest began the vows: "Do you, Laura Lillian Gidney, take this man, Clarence Keith Baird, to be your husband, to have and to hold, from this day forward, for richer for poorer, for better or worse..." I hesitated for a moment, but then whispered, "I do!"

On our way to the wedding reception, we drove through Bear River with horns honking loudly and people waving. In the Hall, a reception line was formed and the hundred guests greeted us; most of them were Clarence's relatives and friends. My relatives were few and far between but my father's mother, "Grammy Mabel", was there with a big smile. Everything about her was big, including her heart.

My friend's mother provided entertainment by playing lovely old familiar songs on the piano while we danced. Delicious refreshments were served and we finally cut our three-tier wedding cake which everyone seemed to enjoy. Clarence and I made a brief exit so that I could change from my wedding dress into "my going-away outfit", a dark red suit and royal blue sequined hat and gloves. Mom had said that it was the proper thing to do, and I wanted to be "proper". It did seem strange to dress up so, when in fact we were only going a few miles away that night.

Clarence had made a reservation in a motel in Annapolis. Far from being a "bridal suite", it was a small room with bed, bath and little else. This was the first time that Clarence and I were completely on our own, with no one to fear, no one to interrupt or catch us. We were husband and wife and whatever we did was legal. I should have no inhibitions now. I had packed a beautiful long blue negligee on which my mother had sewn pink marabou fur trim. I thought Clarence would compliment me and say how beautiful I looked, but his reaction was, "Where the hell did you get *that*?" Being very tenderhearted, I was stunned and my feelings were hurt. I wanted to cry and he offered no comfort. He just said, "Don't be so touchy!" My romantic mood was crushed. This was our wedding night and I knew Clarence wanted to have sex. I wanted and needed some tender and sweet words but there weren't any—and I just smiled. We made "love" but without any passion. It was his "due" and he took advantage of it. It was over as quickly as he wanted—but not quick enough for me.

Where were the magical feelings of passion, warmth, heat and desire I had heard about? Was this it? Is this what I had heard the girls talking about? Is this what they put in the romance magazines? I'm afraid the stars disappeared from my eyes that night. Did I really even have to be there? For all Clarence seemed to care, he could have been making love to the mattress. Perhaps things would change as we grew to know each other. I had a lot of learning to do.

The next day we left on the Digby ferry to New Brunswick. We were on our way to Ste. Anne de Bellevue in

Quebec, where Clarence would attend MacDonald College to complete his degree in Agricultural Science.

We moved into what they called "The Huts", an old residence on campus for married couples. Huts were long rows of housing connected together where we shared a bathroom with a couple living next to us. We shared with a couple from India. The rent was only $25 a month—thankfully, since Clarence would not be working.

Our first morning in the Huts, I got up early and was excited to prepare a special breakfast for my husband. I set the table properly with a beautiful lace tablecloth and dishes that had been wedding gifts. It looked exactly as I thought it should for our "first breakfast" in our new home. I could hardly wait for Clarence to get up. I heard him as he came into the room and I waited for his praise.

"Now there's something I don't like!" he said.

It sounded like he was upset with me and I asked him what he meant.

"The table looks stupid that way," he complained, and added, "Why are you so foolish?"

I hadn't expected to be reprimanded for my efforts. I had to learn not to be "so touchy".

I soon discovered that there were many cockroaches in the huts. I didn't recognize what they were at first since I had never seen one. I would spray and they would leave, only to return again when someone else sprayed, I supposed. Being very conscious about hygiene and cleanliness, I realized I had no other choice but to do my best to keep the place clean, in spite of the cockroaches.

Since I was able to speak French I got a job in the Bank of Montreal as a teller at $2,000 a year. It was enough to support us.

I realized that our life in the bedroom wasn't going to improve on its own. If I was going to be happy about lovemaking, I had to do something. I bought a book called "All About Sex" and asked Clarence to read it with me. His response was, "If you have to read a book, there's something the matter with you!" I was hurt and didn't mention it to him again, although I did read it. I decided to try one of the ideas recommended in the book and hoped to introduce some excitement into our lovemaking. I sprayed whipped cream on my breasts. When Clarence saw me he said, "Don't be so god-dammed foolish!" He never needed any foreplay or romance and didn't seem to care whether I did or not.

As time went on I began to ask myself, "When did I sign up to gather beer bottles?" I gathered them at home almost every morning. What part of my marriage vows said that? Was it the "for better or worse" part? I had been so naïve about living with a man, especially one that drank. Not that people drinking around me was anything new. My mother always had a glass of beer in her hand or at least within reach. This was different—it seemed that Clarence enjoyed beer even more than my mother did.

We received visitors from Nova Scotia—my mother and her boyfriend Mac, my sister Carmen, Clarence's mother and brother, who all arrived in Ste. Anne de Bellevue. The first night they were there Mom and Florence got into an argument and Mom, Mac and Carmen left. They drove to my Aunt Isabel's in Quebec. They were only there a short time before my mother and Aunt Isabel got into an argument and they left again. Clarence's mother and brother stayed with us for a few days and then returned home by themselves.

About a month later, I received a call from my sister Carmen. I could tell she was in tears.

"What's the matter, Carmen?" I was concerned.

"I am going to die...*sniff...sniff*... I'm not going... *sniff... sniff*..."

"What do you mean?" I was even more concerned now.

"Mom said she is sending me away to a Home... a Catholic School for girls... in New Brunswick... with the nuns. I will have to live there. I hate her."

Mom had frequently threatened me with "I'll put you in a home, little girl!" whenever she wanted to scare me, so I figured she was doing the same to Carmen.

"She's probably just trying to frighten you and she really won't do that."

"Yes, she will. She said that she has already enrolled me at the College Notre Dame d'Acadie and that I'd better pack my clothes and that she wasn't going to put up with me anymore... and that I'd better be ready by the weekend because... *sniff...sniff*... because she and Mac are driving me there on Sunday."

"And, what about Aunt Thelma and Uncle Hubert? What do they say?"

"Mom said she doesn't care what they say... that I am *her* daughter and she will do what *she* wants with me. She came to their place last week and got into a fight with Aunt Thelma... and took me out of there... and brought me to Bear River."

"Oh Carmen, I am so sorry and I wish I knew what to do for you. I know it won't do any good to talk to Mom." And

45

I knew it wouldn't. "You'll be better off away from Mom anyway and out of that place. And once you get to the college, you might love it. I hear that it is a wonderful school."

"I guess... maybe... and at least I won't have to live with Mom."

Carmen did attend the College and lived there for the next two years. I received letters from her saying she had made new friends and it wasn't as bad there as she had been afraid it would be.

Clarence had many male "buddies" at MacDonald College. My only friends were his buddies' wives who usually lay on blankets outside in their bathing suits trying to get a tan. I wasn't going to show myself in a bathing suit and made up some sort of excuse like "housework". They all drank and parties developed into pranks; like running back and forth on top of the hut roofs. Once, our Volkswagen was lifted onto the top step of the girls' residence; another time someone's bed was thrown out of a top story window.

Our first wedding anniversary arrived and I prepared Clarence's favourite roast beef dinner. I fought the urge to set the table the "proper" way because I knew that a fancy table would only upset him again. With soft music playing, candles lit and a bottle of wine, it was a romantic setting. I wanted this evening to be perfect. His gift of a new watch was wrapped, his card was signed "With Love, on Our First Anniversary".

When he arrived home Clarence looked somewhat disheveled in his work clothes from a field trip. He went straight to the fridge and got himself a beer, and sat down at the table for supper. He reached into his back pocket and pulled out an envelope and said, "Here," surprising me with a card.

"A card!" I exclaimed, "How thoughtful."

I opened the envelope and took out the card. There was a drawing of a little girl holding an umbrella in the rain. Inside, the verse read, "Happy Anniversary – Rain or Shine, Hope It's Fine." I smiled and thanked him but I felt he had rained on my parade. It was a start though, and romantic or not, at least he had remembered. I would look forward to the next card. Unfortunately, this turned out to be the pattern for all my special occasions.

We were in Ste Anne de Bellevue until Clarence finally graduated with a Bachelor of Science in Agriculture degree. He had decided he wanted to go to Acadia University in Wolfville, Nova Scotia, and enrolled in their Bachelor of Education program.

In the summer of 1962, we moved into an apartment in New Minas, within a short distance to Acadia University. It was a beautiful campus surrounded by huge trees and manicured lawns where students sat to read, study or just sit in groups to talk. I envied them. But I would still need to work while Clarence got his education, and so I found a job at the Bank of Nova Scotia in Kentville. I started as a teller but within a few months was promoted to Loans Officer.

In December that year, I began to feel nauseated daily. I was sure I had the flu but it just wouldn't go away. Facing a day at work was becoming difficult. A visit to the doctor discovered the reason for the constant nausea—I was pregnant. Hopefully the nausea would settle and I could get through my workdays. But it didn't, and I had no choice but to leave my job. Within a few weeks I was completely dehydrated from vomiting and "would have to be hospitalized for intravenous feedings", the doctor said. I would need some help getting through this, but it seemed that Clarence was not prepared to offer any. A decision was made that I be admitted to the Digby Hospital near Bear River. So once again, I returned to Bear River to stay with my mother; but I knew she was a great nurse and would treat me kindly as long as I was sick. Clarence moved out of our apartment and found a place to board while he finished his studies. I saw him on the weekends when we would stay at his mother's place.

On completion of his Bachelor of Education degree Clarence was hired to teach at the local Academy. We decided to buy Clarence's family home on a 100-acre farm in a little village called Greenland. We made an arrangement with Clarence's mother that she and her twelve-year-old son Keith would live with us while we built her a new little bungalow. Her house was being built gradually as we could afford the materials for it.

It was not easy living with Florence's outspoken ways. We were living in what had been her home, and trying to make this our home was difficult. I wanted to hang my curtains, I wanted to replace her dishes with my own, I wanted to have private discussions with my husband. Impossible! My husband was her son and whatever he did was fine with her. I was outnumbered. Once, when I was cooking a turkey, she phoned a neighbour to see if they had any poultry seasoning as she was making the dressing. I overhead her words: "Clarence likes dressing the way his mother makes it!"

I was expecting my first child at the end of August and still suffered badly from nausea. One night I was awake all through the night throwing up. No one was showing any concern as I trudged up and down the narrow stairway to the bathroom. Finally, Clarence yelled, "Jesus Christ mom, aren't you going to do anything?" He wasn't about to offer any help, but I was disturbing his sleep. Finally, it was decided that I should go to Bear River to my mother's place. I was put to bed there and the doctor was called. I was vomiting green bile and taken to the hospital to start intravenous feedings once more. I was totally dehydrated. The intravenous feeding managed to stop my vomiting but only for a few days. The doctor prescribed anti-nausea drugs. It was during the time that thalidomide was being prescribed but I thank the Good Lord I was not given that drug. I returned to Bear River where my mother cared for me for a couple of weeks. I was very weak and could barely walk up and down the stairs. I had lost eleven pounds in one week, but returned to our home in Greenland. I was extremely ill during my pregnancy and was hospitalized three times for intravenous feedings.

In the summer of 1963 the bungalow was completed. Florence and Keith finally moved out and into their new home. I breathed a sigh of relief.

On August 29th 1963, I was twenty-one and nine months pregnant. Not a card, not a letter, not a gift, and not a cent of support, but my father appeared out of nowhere with his wife Charlotte and arrived at our house. I had for so long thought about my father and wished that I could see him again. Now here he was. What was there to say? I only saw him a few times after that. His wife seemed to be jealous of any time we might have together.

I went to the hospital with labour pains the next day and my baby was born. Perhaps the shock of my father turning up brought on the birth!

Thus, on August 30, 1963, a beautiful and healthy little girl made her first appearance in the world. We named her Lisa Lynn. She was adorable. Did it surprise me that my father did not come to see his first grandchild?

I was twenty-one and felt so ill-prepared to be a mother, but I was devoted to my little baby girl and loved every minute with her.

The house was not insulated and in the winter months it was freezing cold. Situated on a high hill, there was nothing to keep the cold winds from blowing through, especially with no storm windows. Our heat came from a wood furnace and a floor grate in the dining room was one of the few places to get warm. Would frozen water in the toilet bowl or the mats frozen to the floor qualify as being too cold?

It had been a wild stormy night with the wind howling through the old house. I awoke to a vision standing at the foot of my bed. It was in a long gown with arms outstretched, holding a pillow and reaching. I screamed: "Oh My God!" Was I having a nightmare? The figure laughed. "I was trying to stuff the pillow into the broken window." It was my mother-in-law, Florence, who had stayed overnight to baby-sit. She said, "I didn't want to wake you."

I took Baby Lisa for a visit to Bear River to see Mom and Grammy Lil. Carmen had returned from her studies at the

College and I wanted her to see my sweet little baby girl. Carmen drew me aside and started to cry.

"What's wrong, Carmen?"

"I can't stay here with her," she sobbed. "It's like living in hell."

How well I knew what it was like. "I will talk to her."

"It won't do any good… you know it won't. You know what she's like. I can't stay here. I want to go and live with you. Oh please, please, take me with you… today!" She was right! It wouldn't do any good to talk about it, and I couldn't leave her with Mom any longer. When I suggested it to Mom, she flew into a rage. "Who do you think you are, little girl, coming into this house and telling me that you are taking Carmen to live with you? She is my daughter and I will do what I want with her. Get the hell out of here!"

I left, but Carmen left with me. She was going to live with Clarence and I and we would give her a home until she finished her high school. It was good to have some help at home and Carmen pitched in to make my life easier, sometimes baby-sitting with Lisa.

Clarence decided he wanted to have farm animals and soon our barn housed numerous cattle, pigs, and chickens. My workload was increasing as each morning I had to feed the animals, clean out the stalls, and place fresh straw for their beds. I hated the smell of manure; although it did seem to fade the longer I was in the barn. Once back in the house, I realized that the smell was still in my clothes; my hair and body also reeked of it. Each time I had to bath and change into fresh clothes. Sometimes Carmen would don barn clothes and give me a break with the chores.

Clarence was still teaching at the Academy and had decided he wanted to take a "Counselor" program at Acadia

University. He would attend for four summers. I would find out later that during this time he had met a lady named Barbara Wilmott who was also attending the University. I didn't know it at the time, but she would figure prominently in our future, especially his.

My Aunt Isabel still lived in Saint Eustache with my Uncle Donald. A call came that she was very ill, so my mother and Aunt Margaret set off to bring her back to Bear River. She had developed cirrhosis of the liver from her alcoholism. She had been a beautiful and very kind woman; more like my grandmother than any of the others. But now she was skin and bones and she couldn't walk.

Her alcohol was limited to a tiny portion daily and gradually her health began to improve. My mother was a great nurse and once again I had to give her credit for the care she provided when someone was ill. As Aunt Isabel's condition improved, she wanted to return to her home and husband in Quebec; and so she did. Within a very short time she passed away at 46 years of age. Her body was shipped back to Nova Scotia and she was buried next to her father in Weymouth cemetery; without a tombstone. We never heard from her husband again; Aunt Isabel used to call him her "little blue-eyed boy". I thought she was much too good for him.

Seven months after Lisa was born, nausea alerted me to the fact that I was pregnant again. The doctor confirmed my suspicions and a second baby was due in December 1964. Once again nausea was a daily occurrence and necessitated intravenous feedings to settle my stomach for a few days. On a snowy winter day after errands I returned home to find our long driveway was completely blocked with new snow and I would have to walk through the drifts to get to the house. With a huge belly and less than good balance, I put one foot into the snow and sat down, lifted the other foot out and stepped ahead. It seemed to me like our quarter-mile long driveway had lengthened.

Carmen had now graduated from High School and moved to the city with several other girl friends to find a job. She would arrive home occasionally for a visit and was always dressed in the finest fashions. Her wardrobe soon included a beautiful fur coat, a sharp contrast to the old one I wore.

She was a "city girl" now and even her manner of speaking was changing. Country folk would call it "putting on airs". Carmen had always been very dramatic but now she was becoming more so.

On December 23, 1964, I had another beautiful little girl and we named her Julie. She was adorable with those beautiful blue eyes and long eyelashes. Lisa was sixteen months old.

Four months later, I was expecting my third child and hospitalized for intravenous feedings once more due to nausea. Dr. Thompson agreed to tie my tubes during a Caesarean delivery.

I was nine months pregnant when my dear Grammy Lil died of heart failure. Grammy Lil used to play "Oh Dem Golden Slippers", which went,

> Oh, dem golden slippers
> Oh, dem golden slippers
> Golden slippers I'se goin' to wear
> To walk the golden street!

Ironically, I had bought my grandmother a pair of golden slippers for Christmas but she passed away before she had a chance to open her gift. This was in mid-December, 1965. I knew she was now able to walk "Those Golden Streets"— with or without those slippers!

My mother and Aunt Margaret tried to persuade me not to attend her funeral but nothing could keep me away. I had lost the greatest lady in my life. There would never be another like her and I felt a tremendous loss. Grammy Lil had always said that when she died her daughters would just bury her and not even place a tombstone on her grave. She was right. Not that they couldn't afford it, but money for alcohol was more important to them. When I attended the burial, the gravesite contained a weathered wooden cross with the names of my grandfather and his only son roughly carved on it. Grammy Lil was buried beside them in an unmarked grave. She deserved so much more. I vowed to change that for her.

Years later I used my own money to purchase a beautiful tombstone for the unmarked graves in Weymouth. Unable to get the necessary information for the tombstone from the family, I went to the Weymouth Catholic Church and spoke to the priest. He was able to find the records of birth and death. I had my grandfather and grandmother's names carved on the tombstone, as well as their young son's name and my Aunt Isabel's. Grammy Lil could rest now. I loved her so and she was my idol. I invited my mother, Aunt Margaret, and Aunt Thelma to donate towards the tombstone. Aunt Margaret sent me a cheque for $100.

Little Elizabeth was born Jan. 18, 1966. She was adorable and precious, especially since she was to be my last pregnancy—or so I thought.

Chapter Four

Surprised by Pain...and Joy

One day, almost a year after Elizabeth was born, I began to have terrible pains in my stomach and told Clarence. He decided to head for the Legion anyway. The pains became increasingly unbearable and I phoned Clarence at the Legion. He rushed me to the hospital and when I arrived there I had to be carried in since I couldn't stand up.

An emergency surgery resulted and it was discovered I had a three-week pregnancy in my tube. One ovary had ruptured and the bleeding had gone down into my leg. I returned home to care for three young babies, doing my best to recover from another incision in my abdomen.

Within a year nausea alerted me to the symptoms of yet another pregnancy in spite of my tubes being tied and having only one ovary. A visit to the doctor confirmed that I was indeed pregnant again and that this pregnancy appeared normal. I was three months pregnant and starting to feel somewhat better, when Clarence and I with another couple set out on a trip to visit his Uncle Wilfred in Greenwood. Everyone else was drinking and laughing. I was starting to get bad cramps.

When we arrived at Wilfred's home everyone was talking, laughing and drinking more. I asked where the washroom was. Everyone sobered up quickly when, as I stood in the middle of their kitchen, about a quart of bright red blood spilled out of me onto the floor.

They tried to reach a doctor but couldn't, so I was put onto the back seat of Wilfred's car and we headed for the Middleton Hospital. Clarence and Wilfred went inside but came back out to say they had been told it was Apple Blossom Festival time and there wasn't a doctor in town. We headed for Annapolis Royal hospital. I was in labour. By the time we arrived at the hospital the doctors were preparing for someone else's emergency surgery. It was decided that mine was more urgent. I remember telling Clarence to "look after the girls" as I was taken to the operating room and wondered if I would ever see them again.

I awoke from surgery to learn that I had had an emergency hysterectomy. I was told that the baby had been pushing a hole through the uterus and that I had come extremely close to dying. The doctor said, "If the uterus had ruptured, as it could have done with a sudden jar, you might have had twenty minutes to live."

I returned home with stitches in my abdomen once more. There were three little girls to care for and Clarence offered no help. The children were my responsibility.

My days were busy with housework. I had no luxuries like an automatic washer or dryer. Diapers were made of cloth and laundry had to be done daily. The old wringer washer had to be filled with a hose attached to the kitchen sink. Once the clothes were washed, the washer had to be drained with a bucket and then refilled for the rinse cycle. After the wringer broke, I had to wring clothes out by hand. Clothes had to be hung outside on the clothesline at the back of the house. Winters were the hardest as I pried clothes off the line and brought them in to thaw over the furnace grate in the dining room. Of course the wood furnace had to be tended in order to dry the clothes and keep the house warm.

My life was not easy but I had the joy of my three little girls. They were a delight as they played together and only occasionally got into mischief. Lisa was like a little mother with the other two. They all helped with folding the clothes and putting their own away in their bureau drawers. They loved to play with water in the kitchen sink so I arranged for them to have some plastic dishes to wash and told them how helpful they were.

I entertained them with "make-up" games. I cut different lengths of yarn and showed them how to make pictures on the rug. I sprayed whipped cream on the tabletop and let them do some finger painting. They dressed up in some grown-up clothes and pretended they were ladies. In the summer they had tea parties on the front verandah. They made up names for themselves and invited me to "tea". I would give myself an imaginary name like "Mrs. Brown." We acted out our little drama with me being invited to come for tea and cookies.

Their birthdays were special events and we celebrated by inviting friends and having a party. I decorated little trees with paper-wrapped suckers and balloons. The girls thought that was so exciting!

Elizabeth was extremely talkative and tormented the other two. As soon as her little eyes opened, so did her mouth. She would say, "Lisa, are you awake?" and "Julie, are you awake?" over and over until they finally were.

They would amuse themselves with wrapping small presents for me. All they needed was paper and lots of scotch tape; then they would excitedly bring me my gifts, sometimes a pencil, sometimes a spool of thread. I always exclaimed how surprised I was and how thoughtful they were and how much I loved the presents.

Our only social activity together as a couple was going to dances. Clarence and I loved to dance and were especially good together doing the "jive." Of course, Clarence and the friends we attended with always drank, and usually quite heavily. Yet they drove. There were always bottles of liquor and paper cups in the car and everyone except me drank on the way to the dance. Bottles were frequently tossed from the windows. It was a night out and, in spite of the drinking, I looked forward to it.

In 1966 my mother and "Mac" decided to get married and I offered to have the wedding and reception at our place. It was not an easy task but I managed to decorate our archway with wedding bells and fern plants, and to bake for the reception. It turned out beautifully and I hoped that at last my mother would be happy with her new husband and life in his home.

Carmen had become engaged to a young man from Bear River and their wedding date was set for the fall of 1967. She was still working in Halifax but they were to be married on the military base nearby. I assumed the role of "Mother of the Bride" and proceeded to make all the arrangements for the wedding. That included the church, the priest, the hall, the photographer, the cake, the refreshments and the gowns; the gowns were to be made by a local dressmaker. Carmen would deal with the invitations. Their wedding day arrived and Carmen looked absolutely beautiful in her long flowing white gown and veil. She looked as glamorous as any bride I had ever seen.

I decided to join the "Valley Drama group" and was finally taking part in an activity I enjoyed outside of the home. Memorizing lines in plays was easy for me and so I played one of the lead roles in Noel Coward's *Fallen Angels*.

Chapter Five

Precious Lord, Take My Hand

Centennial year was in 1967 and to celebrate the occasion, in 1968 Nova Scotia Light and Power completed their replica of a grist mill in Lequille.

The construction project was the Lequille River hydro station, which generated about 15,000 horsepower for peak load purposes. It was built on the site of Poutrincourt's grist mill, which was set up in the spring of 1607, near Port Royal, Nova Scotia. It was the first water mill on the North American Continent and the Lequille River was the first to be harnessed by the European settlers. The exterior of the modern power station is a replica of a French mill of the seventeenth century, but the station houses machinery capable of turning out more than 150 times more horsepower.[1]

My drama group was to be involved in a historical re-enactment commemorating early French settlement in Nova Scotia, specifically the signing of a treaty between Champlain and the Micmac Indians at Lequille in Annapolis County. I was an Indian Maiden and appeared on the cover of the Nova Scotia Light and Power magazine with another actor. Canadian Broadcasting Corporation produced a 16 mm colour film of the pageant, which is on file in Nova Scotia Archives and Records Management in Halifax. The film was called "Return to Lequille – Where History Was Made."

Clarence's mother was our baby-sitter during these times when I had to be away during rehearsals and performances, or when we went out together and I have to admit that she was the best. The girls loved her as she did them. She couldn't help but spoil them and they loved it. The house was usually a mess when we arrived home, but I knew the children had been in safe hands. Clarence would sometimes exclaim, "For Christ's sake Mom, it looks like a God-dammed cyclone hit this place!" The diaper pail would be in the middle of the kitchen floor, while used Kleenex was piled on the countertop alongside half eaten apples. The house would be in disarray. It fell to me to put things back in order.

However there were many times that Florence irritated me with her interfering and outspoken ways. One day she came into the house and proceeded to get a bucket of water, took up all my mats, and scrubbed the floors with a brush. I had just scrubbed and waxed, but she said, "We can't have you

---

[1] See "NOVA SCOTIA LIGHT AND POWER COMPANY, LIMITED" at
http://www.lib.uwo.ca/business/ccc-novascotialight.htm

slipping on that waxed floor with the babies." I wanted to keep the peace so never confronted her about anything.

We had carpeting in our living room, a cheap kind with foam backing. One day I noticed it was covered with numerous creepy crawly sow bugs. They were coming up from the dirt basement! I was at a loss what to do when the milkman arrived at the door. The girls rushed to tell him: "We have bugs!" Not too embarrassing, I guess!

The basement was sprayed and thankfully the carpet was removed. I had hated that orange carpet anyway so was relieved to see it gone.

I had been given my Grammy Lil's piano and started taking piano lessons again. It was my entertainment and my comfort. I played hymns over and over again and this became my prayer time. One day I was asked if I would be willing to play in church. I was not feeling at all confident about my musical ability but finally agreed. I would always find out what the hymns were going to be on Sunday and then practice them over and over again. My right hand would frequently make mistakes when it reached for the keys, but I learned to compensate with my left hand and covered the mistakes. As I became more experienced I became more confident and soon was playing for Sunday school, and even played for funerals and weddings. It seemed I was spending more and more time at church, nearly always taking my children along. On Sundays we were up early and off the girls and I went.

Clarence never came with us. He was either sleeping off a hangover from the night before, or up and drinking with his buddies who had already gathered at our place—our door was never locked. Usually I had to clean up the beer bottles and caps in the kitchen before I left for church.

Our new minister at the Baptist Church was Larry Boone. He and his family—wife Alice, teenage daughter Melissa, and two young sons, Mathew and Timothy—had moved into the parsonage. Mr. Boone was a handsome man, so full of life and energy and so well groomed. He was also extremely charismatic and each Sunday his sermons were well received. He seemed to be able to persuade church members to do whatever he asked.

Mr. Boone was still in the military but was a Licentiate and taking Divinity courses at Acadia University for a retirement career. The congregation grew, as did the "spirit" in the church. Soon we formed a music group and I played the piano with Willard on the guitar and Joanne on the harpsichord. We loved to play and sing the old hymns and frequently held concerts and hymn sings in various churches. My faith grew and prayer became a part of our gatherings. I became extremely fond of Mr. Boone and saw him as a very spiritual person, one to be trusted. I confided in him about my life at home with Clarence and asked him to pray for me.

My mother and I had not been speaking for some time due to one of our many "fallings out" and I was upset. I was very unhappy with my husband's lifestyle, and I was worn down physically as well as emotionally. As usual I sat at my piano and played hymns for comfort. I was playing "Precious Lord, Take My Hand" and crying at the same time. The phone rang and it was my mother phoning to talk as if nothing had happened that had caused us to be at odds. I knelt beside my piano bench to give thanks and then continued to play the same hymn. As if by magic, I felt the greatest sense of peace come over me. I seemed to see a vision of Christ and all was well with the world. I could not explain how I felt now except that I was renewed with a sense of well-being. All fear was gone and all I felt was love.   The peace I was experiencing had to be the Holy Spirit.

The Bible that had been gathering dust on the table had not been read except with logic, not fervour. Now I craved reading it, and each time I read it with new understanding. It gave me new life, and I wanted to talk openly about it. I had only religion before but knew that I had salvation now—what a tremendous distinction! I wanted to tell others about Christ and witness to them. I spoke in church about my experience and compared myself to the wicked witch in "Sleeping Beauty" who would look into her mirror and say, "Mirror, mirror on the wall, who's the fairest of them all?" The mirror would reply, "You are." But then I had looked in the mirror and discovered that I was not the fairest of them all and saw my true self, a creature who now had a new way of looking at myself and the world. I was "re-born" and had salvation. Praise the Lord! I finally knew true faith and new calmness.

♣

Suddenly my path and my plan became clear. I would no longer stay with my husband. Armed with only an $18.00 Children's Allowance cheque and the clothes on my back, I gathered the children and asked my mother and her husband "Mac" to come for us. We left for Halifax that day and arranged for my sister Carmen and her husband David to meet us there. We would stay with them until I could find work and a place for us to live. How naïve I was and how ill-prepared. Clarence had arrived home after work to find us gone and he had no idea where we were. Carmen must have phoned him as it wasn't very long before he arrived, looking very humble. He begged me to go back home, and said "things" would change. He convinced me and I agreed.

Things did change for a while and Clarence spent more time with the children. That didn't last long and soon things returned to the way they were before, with Clarence drinking and spending his time with his buddies at the Legion.

I decided I should try to further my education and enrolled at Acadia University for a degree program. Maybe subconsciously I knew I wanted to be better prepared to support myself and the children, should the need arise again. I wrote my GED exams to obtain a Grade XII equivalency and passed. I attended Acadia the next two summers and in the winter attended evening classes to obtain more credits. We hired a young girl to live-in and baby-sit during the summer classes. My schedule was more than hectic as I rose at 5 a.m., did whatever housework needed to be done at home, and drove an hour and a half to attend classes from 8 a.m. until noon. When I arrived home I would attend to the children and the house, prepare supper, bath and settle the children into bed. Then from 8 p.m. until midnight, sometimes later, I would do my assignments, studying and writing papers. I was usually operating on four hours sleep. Somehow I managed to pass all my courses and was gradually building towards my degree. I was beginning to feel as though I wasn't really so stupid after all.

Clarence had purchased an old boat and one day he and his friends were on it when the tide went out, leaving them stranded on the mud flats. He arrived home late that night, dirty and with a cut foot—he had stepped on broken glass. I bathed his foot, treated the wound and put him to bed to sleep it off. When I went to bed I couldn't help but think of the many times I had lain beside Clarence while he reeked of liquor coming through his pores.

I reminded Clarence that for the good of our marriage we really needed to have something in common, but to no avail. One night after he had arrived home drunk and I had helped him up the steps to bed, he lay snoring. I had orange nail polish on my toenails and more in the bottle. I got up and proceeded to paint his toenails to match mine. Morning came and I woke to the sound of Clarence hollering from the downstairs bathroom: "What the hell!" He had gone for a morning pee and had gazed down. I started to laugh and hollered, "We FINALLY have something in common!" The children were awake and so I shared my practical joke with them. Elizabeth yelled to her father: "You'd look good in a tutu, dad!"

Another anniversary arrived and we had planned to go out for dinner to celebrate. I got dressed up but Clarence didn't arrive home until late that evening. He was drunk and had a bottle in his pocket. He was staggering and his speech was slurred when he said he was ready to go out to dinner and that he would drive. I refused to go. I did not want to be in the car when he had another accident, like the time he was drinking and rolled the car over three times. Somehow he came out unscathed. I thanked God that the children weren't with him that day and that no one had been walking on the highway. I feared that it was just a matter of time before it happened again.

One fine day, Clarence promised us that he would take us swimming. He had been out drinking and arrived home saying he was ready to take us for our day at the beach. We had a Volkswagen at the time and the three girls, the dog and I got into the car and off he drove. When we arrived at the beach, Clarence continued on down the narrow walking path instead of parking in the lot above. He drove onto the beach, not slowing down. I was begging him to stop but he wouldn't! He kept driving right into the water and we were getting deeper. Either the car stalled or he did stop, finally. I managed to push the door open and the dog was swimming for his life. I was up to my waist in water and reached for the girls, holding on to them as tightly as I could. They were screaming and I was numb as I waded to the beach. Clarence managed to open his door and waded through the water. I wasn't concerned whether he made it to safety or not.

Once on the beach, Clarence wanted to know why we didn't want to go swimming. We walked to the road and stopped a car going by. Our car was full of salt water and had to be towed to a garage.

How much longer could I deal with this lifestyle?

Chapter Six

Escape – Or a Downward Spiral?

After serving for four years as our Baptist minister, Mr. Boone announced one Sunday morning that he would be leaving. I was devastated and admitted to myself that I had become dependant on the spiritual comfort and guidance that he was providing me. I also admitted to myself that I had fantasized about him on occasion, imagining how it would feel to hold him close. He was tall, he was dark, and he was handsome. He was the most handsome man I had ever seen. His smile melted my heart. It brought about feelings of desire in me that I had never experienced before.

I decided to visit him at the parsonage and express to him how I felt and tell him that I would miss him terribly. In fact, I admitted to him that I had grown to love him. What was I to do? He suggested we pray together and we did. I felt better.

The next day as I drove past his house and stopped at the Post Office across the street, Mr. Boone came running out and said he wanted to talk to me. He asked to meet me in Middleton for lunch the following day. I was working for Social Services now and would be in that area. We met for lunch and the conversation led to what we had discussed the previous evening. Mr. Boone admitted to having strong feelings for me as well, and said, appearing somewhat embarrassed, "I have to admit that I have often had 'sinful thoughts' about you." We were fearful that this was developing into a situation that could only be disastrous for both of us. We acknowledged that we were both married with families and agreed that we could not allow this to go any further.

I continued to attend church, but could not concentrate on the sermon. Mr. Boone, whom I now thought of as Larry, and I exchanged knowing glances that said, "I know what you're thinking, but this is wrong." Our defenses were gradually weakening. We arranged to meet secretly one afternoon. Within minutes of arriving at our "secret location", we were overtaken with such passion and desire for each other sexually that we were unable to resist making love. I thought, so this is what sex can be like! I was breathless with excitement and experienced feelings and passion like I had never known before. I had been convinced that there was something wrong with me, that I could not enjoy sex—now I knew different. Sex with Larry was like a drug, it was euphoric, and I was addicted. I was sure I was deeply in love, and it had overtaken my feelings and my sensibility. It controlled me.

I had never had sex with anyone except my husband and the guilt was haunting me; as well as the absolute terror of anyone finding out what I had done. Now I could not bring myself to have sex with Clarence and refused his attempts. My loyalties were torn.

My husband was becoming angry and took his frustration out by mistreating our dog. I felt responsible for the punishment being inflicted on the poor innocent animal—he had done nothing wrong and my heart broke for him. I feared that Clarence might eventually do the same to me and I was afraid of him now.

It was the summer of 1974 and my daughters left for a week at Brownie Camp. I knew what I was going to do. I decided to leave Clarence once more, and when the girls returned from Brownie Camp, I would take them and find work and a place for us to live.

I packed a small suitcase and after Clarence left, I found someone to drive me to my mother's place. Things did not go well there and I knew I had to leave. It was getting dark when I left and started walking on the River Road, but I had no idea where I was going. I thought of a motel about three miles away and kept walking. I was crying and singing a song popular at the time: "Here I go, once again, with a suitcase in my hand, I'm walking away down River Road." Exhausted, I finally arrived at the motel and checked in. I had very little money but enough for a couple of nights' accommodation. My friend Gloria came to the motel after I phoned her. I did not tell her about my relationship with Larry but told her only that I was leaving Clarence.

She left and had only been gone for about an hour when Larry arrived at the motel. Gloria had phoned him to say that she was concerned for me and told him where I was. I cried in his arms and he comforted me. "I love you Laura, and I want to be with you. Everything will work out." I didn't know how it would "work out" since he still lived at home. He was still the minister of my church, and he still had a wife and children. As far as anyone knew, he and I were not involved in any way. He would have to deal with that situation in whatever way he felt he needed to. I was not asking him to leave to be with me. I was on my own.

My cousin Marie and husband were visiting from Ontario and after I contacted them they suggested that I could travel back with them for a visit. It seemed like a place to go while I tried to sort out my thoughts and decide on my next step. I had only just arrived in Ontario when a deep depression took hold of me. Being without my children hit me like a ton of bricks and I needed to be with them. The emptiness was unbearable.

I received a phone call from Clarence asking me to come back home. I wanted my children desperately but I did not want to be back with him. I knew I would be branded as a deserter and would be treated as such. Burdened with heavy guilt, I was afraid to go home.

Within a few days, I managed to arrange a flight back to Halifax where I had decided to look for work and a place to live for myself and my girls. I stayed with my sister Carmen and her husband David while I looked for a job. I told them nothing about my affair with Larry. They knew only that I had left Clarence.

It seemed that things would work out when I was hired for the first job I applied for. I had visited an Employment Centre and selected a card from their job bank. I had no idea what the job was and couldn't even pronounce it, but the pay was good. It had to be a "divine sign" when the interviewer's name was Larry Boone, the same name as our

Baptist minister! I was hired immediately as an Expeditor with Hermes Electronics.

I would engage a lawyer and get my children. I didn't doubt for a moment that I would get them; after all, hadn't I been the one who had cared for them, loved them, and taken them to church? Hadn't Clarence been the one who was always drinking and sleeping off hangovers, never spent any time with his family, and never went to church? God *had* to be on my side. He knew that I had been "born again". All those prayers, all that faith—things were going to work out!

I met with a lawyer to begin divorce and custody proceedings. With his assurance that I would have the children, I borrowed $700 for his fee.

Larry phoned Carmen's home to speak with me. She knew him only as "my minister" so suspected nothing untoward when we went out for "coffee". I heard that Clarence's mother had moved into our home. I was afraid to phone the house and had no way of contacting the girls. I ached to see them.

I finally decided to take Carmen into my confidence when on Larry's further visits to Halifax, we wanted to spend more time together. I also wanted to let her know where I was in the event that my daughters needed to contact me so I always left a location and phone number where I could be reached. Little did I know that Carmen was phoning Clarence to pass all of this information on to him!

By now, the town was buzzing with rumours and the shocking news about Larry and me. The rumour was that Larry and I must have been carrying on an affair for the whole time he was ministering there. That was absolutely false but the community would not believe anything else, and there was no way to convince them otherwise. Larry had resigned from the ministry but was still living in the parsonage while he packed to move. His wife had been away on a visit to Alberta with the children and was not yet aware of the rumours.

I was still depressed and taking anti-depressants. The medication made me so sleepy that I could hardly keep my eyes open and frequently had to head for the washroom to try and lay my head down anywhere I could; the only place I could find was against the toilet paper roll.

I was only into my third day's work when Larry arrived at my place of employment. "My wife and children are still away in Alberta visiting her parents," Larry said. "When she returns, I am going to tell her that I am not moving with her, and also tell her the reason why." He added: "I want you to come with me to Cape Breton and live there until I return." Larry wanted to take me to his sister's place in Glace Bay on Cape Breton Island, where I could stay temporarily until things got sorted out.

I felt I had lost all now—my self-respect, my children, my family, my friends, and my self-confidence. I had no one else to turn to, but I knew God had to be on our side; after all, Larry was such a spiritual person and he and I had such great faith. God must have a bigger plan for our lives.

I resigned from my job and left Halifax with Larry. We were on our way to Cape Breton. I had never been there before and had no idea what to expect, but I was with a man that I trusted implicitly. When he held my hand, I felt like nothing could harm me. Being close to him thrilled me and at last I knew what it felt like to be really loved.

Just before we arrived in Glace Bay, Larry slowed the car, pulled into a Provincial Park rest area and turned off the car engine.

"Are you tired?" I asked, thinking that perhaps he was feeling the strain after the long drive.

He gripped the steering wheel tightly, took a deep breath, and then turned to face me. I looked into his eyes trying to understand what was happening. He looked so serious and his tender eyes began to fill with tears. He was silent for a few minutes.

"Is anything the matter Larry? What is it?" I felt anxious. Why had he stopped?

"Well, sweetheart,"—and then he reached over and kissed me, "I have to tell you something… Before we arrive in Glace Bay… you need to know something."

"Know what?" I felt my pulse quicken. What was he going to tell me? That old familiar feeling of fear clutched my heart.

"Well, there's – um – the fact is, there's a nigger in the woodpile."

What did that mean! I waited for him to continue, and I reached for his hand. He smiled, the smile that had captured my heart, the same smile that I first fell in love with when he spoke of God's love and mercy from the pulpit. What could he possibly be going to tell me?

"Larry! Tell me what you mean!" He was frightening me.

He took a deep breath. "My sister – Doreen – she's black."

"She's *black*? What do you mean she's black?" He had to be joking.

He nodded. "And her daughter Lucy too – she's black."

"Oh…okay…" I was confused. Was this all he wanted to tell me? "Is that all?" I asked.

"Well…" I held my breath waiting for him to tell me that he wasn't leaving his wife after all, or that he had changed his mind about me.

"I thought you should know before we get there that Lucy has mental problems. She wears wigs and hears voices." He was scaring me. "She has been in and out of the Nova Scotia Hospital for treatment for her condition. You will find her strange."

"What do you mean by strange, Larry?"

"Well… when you meet her, you'll see. She may stare at you and she might say some weird things."

"Like what?" I was getting unnerved.

"Just silly things, but pay no attention—she's harmless."

"But Larry, you're going to leave me there alone, and now I'm nervous."

"Don't be afraid." He gave me a reassuring smile. "My sister and her husband will know how to handle her." That seemed like small comfort, but if Larry said that I would be all right, then I felt sure I would be.

We arrived at their home and I was shocked to see that his sister Doreen wore white powder all over her black face. She was a big woman, and black, as Larry had said. Why did she have white powder all over her face? I wondered, did she have mental problems also? Doreen's husband was white and even though he was a small man and short, I felt an immediate connection of safety with him. I was introduced to Lucy. She had a look on her face that told me I had best beware: she swore at the imaginary voices that she heard and said, "Murderous, very murderous indeed!" Could I stay here without Larry? I would have to because I had no choice.

Larry stayed with me for two nights before he had to return home to Nova Scotia. He said he would be away for a couple of weeks until he drove to Alberta with his family and see that they were settled. I was somewhat reassured, but feeling worried about what he was to face. I knew his wife was returning shortly from her trip out west and that he was dreading the confrontation with her. I also knew that once he saw his boys again, he was going to be torn apart emotionally and could possibly have a change of heart. He said he would phone me to keep me informed of what was happening, and that evening I waited anxiously for his phone call.

I was relieved when the phone rang and heard Larry's comforting voice. He had arrived back safely. "I miss you Laura," he said, "and I'm lost without you. I love you so much." I needed his reassurance. Just hearing his deep, soft voice aroused me. How could I ever be without him, even for just two weeks? It seemed like an eternity.

It was two days before Larry phoned again. I was shocked when he said, "Alice returned unexpectedly yesterday. Our neighbour met her at the airport and brought her home."

"Why did she come back early?" I was more than curious.

"She said that a neighbour phoned her and told her that there were rumours about you and me. She was livid."

"What does she know?" I wondered what Larry had told her.

"She knows that I am not going to move with her. I told her that I would drive her to Calgary and make sure she and the boys were settled, but that I am going to return to Nova Scotia to be with you."

"Are you sure that is what you want to do, Larry?" I didn't want to hear otherwise but would have to accept his decision if he had changed his mind. I knew the pain of being without one's children.

"Yes, I'm sure. It won't be easy, I know. I am definitely not in love with Alice, but the thought of leaving the children behind is painful." How well I knew what he meant!

"I love you, Laura, and you are so precious to me. I will be in touch often. Please try not to worry."

"I love you too, Larry, and I miss you terribly. Please keep safe."

The next phone call I received from Larry was when he was en route to Calgary. He said that the trip had certainly not been a pleasant one, but they would be arriving at their destination the next day.

"I want you to book a one-way flight to Calgary," he said.

"A one-way flight? Are you saying that you want me to live in Calgary too?"

He chuckled. "No dear, I just want you with me. We will drive back to Cape Breton together. I can't talk for long right now, but I will phone you again tomorrow. Please call the Airlines right away."

I scheduled my flight for that weekend, just two days away. I could hardly wait for Larry to phone so we could make plans to meet at the airport. The day seemed to pass much too slowly as I stared at the telephone waiting for it to ring. Finally, it did. And it was the voice I had been waiting for.

"Larry, I could hardly wait to talk to you. I have booked my flight and I'm scheduled to arrive on Saturday at 6 p.m. on Air Canada Flight Number 872. I couldn't wait to tell you! I'm so excited and anxious to see you again." I waited for Larry to say something.

"That's wonderful, dear!"

I breathed a sigh of relief and realized that even now I had been afraid that he would change his mind. I was always waiting for the unexpected bomb to drop.

"I'll meet you at the airport and reserve a hotel room for us. Tomorrow I will spend the day with the boys and try to explain what is happening. Oh Lord, Laura, I understand better now how you must be feeling without your children. It is gut-wrenching."

"Are you sure you can do this, Larry?" I asked.

"It won't be easy, but I have to face it. God help me!"

Larry met me at the airport as planned. The moment we saw each other we started to run. I was breathless, but it wasn't from running. We held on to each other tightly, but said nothing yet. We were both crying. They were tears of joy, yet I knew the joy was mixed with an unspoken sadness at how we had arrived at this place in our lives.

The next day we left Calgary on the long drive back to Cape Breton Island. It was a four-day drive and it seemed like the honeymoon I had never had.

And so our "new life" began. I told myself that God must have a plan for our lives. Larry was such a spiritual man, after all. Together we would find work and a home so the girls would come and live with us. It was just a matter of time.

We agreed we would have to find jobs and accommodation as soon as possible but we could stay with Larry's sister until we did. Continuing as a minister didn't seem to be appropriate at this time and so Larry would have to look for other employment. He finally found a temporary job selling vacuum cleaners. It was not what he had been used to but it was a start. Since I had banking experience, I applied for a position with the Bank in Glace Bay and was hired right away. Now at least we had a steady income.

We were not in a financial position to be able to afford anything luxurious, or even semi-luxurious, so when we saw a tiny, makeshift trailer for rent we decided, somewhat hesitantly, that it could serve as a temporary shelter at least. The rent was $75 a month and that we could manage. It was a far cry from what we had ever lived in before, but it was a "home". Doreen and her husband agreed to allow us to move the trailer onto their property and hook into their electricity with what seemed like a mile-long extension cord. The bed was nothing more than a sheet of plywood, but with a sleeping bag and blankets, we were somehow able to get a night's sleep. Of course, there was no running water, nor a bathroom. I learned to bathe with a water basin that Larry would carry out to the trailer. We had no choice but to use the bathroom in Doreen's house and many times it was a quick scurry to answer the call of nature. New dishtowels became curtains, but there were only three tiny windows to cover. Somehow I managed to cook meals on a hot plate. Each week I would take everything outside of the trailer and scrub it from top to bottom.

This was far from luxurious living and could have been devastating to many couples. We joked about it, but both of us knew we were feeling humbled by our present living conditions. At least we had each other now but I thought of something that I had once heard Rex Humbard say: "You may get what you want, but you may not want what you get!" Larry sensed what I was thinking and reassured me: "We will move from here into our own place just as soon as we have the money." I knew that we would. Larry had said so.

Women at work were discussing their children and what furniture they were buying. I would not discuss my situation with anyone there, and could not admit the love I felt for my daughters without leaving the door wide open for prying questions.

The trauma of a marriage break-up and the "division" of children is one of the most heartbreaking misfortunes of life. The trauma is intensified for the parent who is without the children, and without the familiar family atmosphere. The world we live in insists on constant reminders of days gone by, and does not allow us to forget the past. Holiday festivities bring thoughts of little ones around the Christmas tree, school concerts, excitement over talking dolls, hockey sticks and sleds... and sadness at the loss of all these things. The "normal" family goes on, seemingly oblivious to those who cry inside. The reminders in our everyday living are not obvious to the families who live day to day in a mother, father, child relationship.

Expressing my feelings in poems sometimes helped me to better understand my thoughts.

> They cannot understand blindness
> Until they fail to see
> They cannot know the feeling
> That's deep inside of me
> Until they've felt the sadness, or
> Until they've known the pain
> Of losing limb, or sight, or child
> Somehow, the pain's the same.

What mother would not have her daughters? Telling anyone would mean that I would be judged as unfit. I was sure of it. And I was beginning to feel that way. I couldn't say that I once also had a home with furniture; I couldn't tell them that now I lived in a trailer with dishtowels for curtains and slept on a piece of plywood.

Winter was fast arriving and it was starting to get cold in the trailer. We would have to find a place that had heat. Since I had left most of my things behind, I also didn't have a winter coat. I shivered with only a sweater, but I could only "window-shop" until I could afford to buy one. Money was still scarce and our salaries only covered the cost of rent, our share of the electricity, groceries and gas for the car. And, we were trying to save enough money to move into better accommodation.

We found an upstairs apartment with low rent and moved into our "new home". With no furniture and meager possessions there was little unpacking to be done. We needed to have at least a place to eat, sleep and sit down. Our landlord offered an old couch we could use and we grabbed the chance. It was an "old couch" all right! But beggars can't be choosers, and so we dragged in a rusty spring couch with no cushions. I covered it with an afghan. We found a card table and chairs at a used furniture shop. Neither of us wanted to sleep on an old bed and so we made our first "major purchase" of a new one. A while back, Larry had bid $100 on a beautiful organ through Crown Assets, and won the bid. It was the organ from a chapel on the Military Base near Bear River. Larry had it delivered to our place—it was beautiful. That completed our furnishings.

At least with the organ, we could have music to cheer us. I would play the old familiar hymns and Larry and I would sing. It was comforting, and would often lead to us kneeling in prayer. We still gave thanks for the things we did have.

Our only other source of entertainment was a radio. The popular songs were often reminiscing of days gone by, sadness, loss of someone, and tear-jerking situations such as "Nobody's Child", Tammy Wynette's "D-I-V-O-R-C-E", and Wayne Newton's "Daddy, Don't You Walk So Fast". Larry and I could relate only too well to the words of the songs and we frequently were in tears.

I longed to hold my children and cried daily, only stopping long enough to go to work. My lawyer had not been in touch with me and I schemed to go to Greenland and take my daughters. I phoned my lawyer and told him what I was planning. He replied, "If you do that, you can be charged with contempt of court." I believed him and resigned myself to waiting it out until I would be awarded custody.

Larry arrived home after work one day with a package. "I stopped at the Liquor Store," he said.

"The Liquor Store? Whatever for?"

He showed me. "It's a bottle of something to make us feel better." It was a bottle of rum—a big bottle. I had seen many bottles of alcohol before but I had never seen it make anyone "feel better". Far from it. It was something that made you drunk and act stupid. Larry brought out two glasses and proceeded to mix us each a drink. He passed me mine.

"Cheers," he said, drinking it down quickly. Then he mixed a second one.

"Cheers," I replied. "This is a new experience for me." I sipped mine slowly and didn't enjoy the taste. If there were a possibility that it would make me feel better though, I'd drink it. Larry seemed to be enjoying his.

"Cheers," he said once more.

"Have you ever drunk before?" I asked him.

"Yes, I have, when I was in the Military, at Mess functions. We always had wine with meals too. The Lord turned the water into wine, you know. We will have to get some wine to go with our dinners."

As the evening progressed, so did the number of drinks we consumed. The drinks were taking effect and my inhibitions were starting to lower. The more we drank, the more we talked; and the more we talked, the more we cried.

The drinking was definitely not making us feel better.

One evening Larry had been drinking heavily as he frequently did lately and had finally lain down on the couch. It was getting late and I thought we should be getting to bed soon since we had to work the next day.

"Larry," I called. No answer. I thought he must be asleep so approached him and gently put my hand on his arm. He didn't stir. I leaned over to give him a kiss, then drew back quickly as I realized he had pills in his mouth.

"Oh my God, Larry! No!" Desperately I reached into his mouth and began to remove pills; his mouth was full of them. He was twisting his head and babbling and he was groggy. I was afraid he had swallowed some of the pills and that this, combined with the alcohol, would prove fatal.

I quickly called the ambulance and went with him to the hospital. They proceeded to check his vital signs. They pumped his stomach. Larry seemed to be coming around.

"Oh Larry, sweetheart, you're going to be okay", I was trying to reassure him.

"What happened?" Larry was becoming alert.

"I thought I had lost you. I love you and need you so much. Everything will be all right."

"I love you too Laura."

We returned home that night and I watched Larry very carefully. I didn't want to let him out of my sight. He needed me as much as I needed him.

For the first time in my life, I went to a fortune teller who told me that I would be moving to a fishing village. Within a couple of weeks, someone at work mentioned that they had a house for rent in a place called Port Morion, a fishing village. The rent was only $100 a month so we grabbed the chance to have a "real home" and moved there immediately. We soon discovered why the rent was so cheap: the place was old, and dilapidated. We were right beside the wharf and the smell of fish was not appealing, but it was a home. Somehow, I turned it into a comfortable one.

My mother phoned me continually, each time complaining that she could no longer care for her husband Mac; he had had a stroke and he required a lot of care. What was she to do? With Larry's agreement, I finally told her that she and Mac could come live with us. We turned our dining room into a bedroom and had a bathroom installed for them downstairs. Before long they arrived.

I had been involved with a drama group and was rehearsing for "The King and I" which required me to be away from home several nights a week. My mother was far from happy about this and within a week she began to complain. "You're never home," she said, and added, "We shouldn't have come!" Within a few days she had arranged for a taxi to take them back to Nova Scotia and left Cape Breton, angry with me.

I did not hear from them until Mom phoned about a year later to say that Mac had died on her birthday, December 15th. He had been living with his daughter Betty in New Brunswick, since Mom had been admitted to Dartmouth Mental Hospital for a period of time. Now she was going to move to Ontario and live with her sister Margaret. I didn't hear from her again for approximately another year.

One night I woke up and Larry was not in bed so I went downstairs to see if he was all right. The house was in darkness but I could hear sounds coming from the basement. As I approached the stairs, Larry was climbing them. I asked what he was doing and he said he must have been sleepwalking. I accepted his excuse and we returned to bed. I laughed about this episode as I related the story to his sister and family. Larry seemed embarrassed and angry at me for talking about it. I didn't understand why until much later.

Chapter Seven

Shattered Illusions

I received word from my lawyer that a court date had been set for my divorce and custody hearing. I thought, "At last I will have my girls with me!"

The long anticipated yet dreaded day arrived. Larry and I arrived at Court and were met by my lawyer. "Your husband is here and has brought the children with him." I wanted to see them. I wanted to hold them. I needed to see and hold them desperately.

"Oh please, can you arrange for me to see them?" I was sure they would be leaving with me that day, but I needed to see them now.

I thought we would be able to meet in a private room but instead the children were brought into the courtroom before the court session began. Our meeting was to be supervised. I broke into tears.

At last, I could see them, hug them, and tell them how much I loved them. But a year had passed and they were confused. They were now 10, 11, and 12. My heart ached as I saw their appearance. They were no longer the well-groomed little girls I had cared for. Julie wore a ragged jacket with a big safety pin where a button should have been. Her expression was sad; my baby girl had been such a happy child and so attached to me. I had caused this hurt and wanted to fix it. But how could I now? Our time together was over much too quickly and I watched as the children left the courtroom. Julie gazed over her shoulder at me and her eyes said, "Please come get me."

I gazed around the courtroom, looking for any of my family or friends. The only ones I saw were Carmen and her husband David. They were sitting in the seats behind us. I had not been in touch with them for a long time but was relieved to see that at least they were there to support me. Maybe the others were waiting outside and would only enter when they were called as witnesses for me.

"What a witch! What a witch," a loud voice said. I thought it sounded like Carmen, but it couldn't be! I turned to see who would say such a thing. Carmen glared at me angrily, and then tilted her chin in the air, just as Mom used to do so frequently. Her husband hung his head.

"What's going on?" I whispered to Larry. He held my hand.

"She just wants attention; she's being her usual dramatic self. Ignore her."

I looked straight ahead and waited for court to begin.

"All rise!" the court clerk said, as a white-haired judge, looking old enough to have been retired for many years, entered.

"You may be seated!" It was the signal that court was about to begin. My heart pounded. I had never been in court before and had no idea what to expect.

I had filed for mental cruelty and Clarence had counter-filed for abandonment.

I had given my lawyer pages of notes describing incidents in detail; the drinking, the broken promises, ignoring the children, the selfishness, the time he had driven the car into the ocean with the children and I, the lack of feeling for me or the children; enough, I thought, to prove mental cruelty. I had also made a list of people who I believed would be willing to support me with these "allegations."

Clarence's lawyer began to call his witnesses. I watched in shock as Carmen left her seat to take the stand and was sworn in. She placed her hand on the Bible, probably the first time she had ever been that close to one.

"Do you swear that the information you shall give shall be the truth, the whole truth, and nothing but the truth?"

"I do!" she said and sat down very demurely, yet dramatically.

"Okay," I thought, "she is going to tell the truth, so that should help me, not hurt me." But why was she a witness for Clarence?

"State your name."

" Carrrrrrrrr-men Rrrri-ta Rrrrr-ice," she said, rolling her R's and pronouncing each word clearly.

"Mrs. Rice, do you know Laura Baird?"

She gazed at me in an unfriendly way. "Yes, I most certainly do. She is my sister, I'm sorry to say."

I couldn't believe my ears! What was she up to? And why would she be doing this to me? I turned to look at her

88

husband and he hung his head again. We had been such good friends and I had to believe he didn't approve.

"Are you aware that in 1974 Laura left her three little children and that their father Clarence has been caring for them?"

"Yes, I know. I have tried to do everything that I possibly could for them, the poor little things. Clarence has taken good care of them and been wonderful to them as I knew he would."

'*What*!' I asked myself.

"And, are you aware that Laura has been living with a Larry Boone, a *former* minister who left his family also?"

"Oh yes, indeed I am. I think it is *ab-so-lute-ly* disgusting. How any mother could just up and leave her children and run away to be with her *lover...well...* in my opinion, any woman who would do *that* is unfit!" She seemed to spit the words out as she raised her eyebrows and shook her head.

"Did Laura stay with you and your husband in Halifax for a period of time after she left her family?"

"Yes, she did. I really didn't want to have her there but my husband talked me into it, saying that we had lots of room. We live in a beautiful house of course, and there are three guest rooms. We frequently entertain with David's career, you know, and with Laura there I was embarrassed to think I might have to discuss her with my friends. I was thrilled to see her finally leave."

I could not believe what she was saying. This was the person I had taken into my home while she finished school. This was the person I had cared for. How could she be doing this to me? Why?

"Do you know where Laura went after she left your home?"

"Well, she did contact me by phone with places and phone numbers and asked me to let her know if her children phoned. But why would I do that? The children were better off without her!"

"Did you keep a record of the places and contact numbers?"

"I most certainly did, and I thought Clarence should know, so I told him."

My jaw dropped. I was stunned.

"Thank you Mrs. Rice. You may step down."

Carmen rose, turned to Clarence's lawyer and smiled. "Thank you sir," she said sweetly. She returned to her seat walking ever so elegantly in her high heels and tailored suit. She had dressed well for the part she was playing, I thought.

The next witness called to the stand was Clarence's mother. I supposed that her age and gray hair would impress the judge.

After she was sworn in, she began her testimony. "I am living with my son Clarence and his daughters and I'm prepared to stay there as long as Clarence needs me."

A third witness entered the courtroom and took the stand. I recognized him as Willard Peck, my fellow musician from church. He testified that he had "never known Clarence to drink". This was a man who had lived in the same community for years and was very well acquainted with Clarence's drinking habits. How could he not know? Yet here he was, having placed his hand on the Bible, having shared so many prayers with Larry and me in our church group, and he was saying that he had "never known

Clarence to drink"? How could he lie like that? And after placing his hand on the *Bible*?

"Unbelievable!" Larry said, as he looked at me in disbelief. I shook my head. It would be an understatement to say that things were not going as I thought they would.

Clarence was called to the stand. He looked well-groomed and although it may not have been obvious to anyone else, I could see the look on his face which I was so familiar with, the look that told me he had been drinking; his mouth always curled up on one side.

When asked what kind of a mother I had been, he unexpectedly replied that I had in fact been a wonderful mother.

'Thank You,' I thought. He was the only one who had a decent thing to say about me.

It was now my lawyer's turn to call witnesses. But where were they? He called not a single witness although I had given him the names of many people in the community. It seemed they had decided not to get involved. After all, this had been Clarence's community; he had been born and raised there. I had been the outsider, even though I had lived there for many years.

I was called to the stand and sworn in. I waited for the questions. By now, I was in a state of shock at not only who Clarence's witnesses had been, but what they had said. This was a living nightmare.

My lawyer asked what seemed to me to be mundane questions. They did not seem to be leading anywhere except establishing who I was, where I lived, who I lived with, and what I did for work.

Clarence's lawyer proceeded with his cross-examination of me. He was breaking me down and I was falling apart.

"And when did you and Larry next COME together?" That was the sarcastic manner of his questions. Everything he said contained insinuations and painted me as a woman who just didn't care about her family.

"All you care about is yourself, isn't that true?"

"No! That's not true? I love my children. It's tearing me apart to be without them. I know they need me."

"Well, your actions prove different, now, don't they? Don't they?"

I was crying so hard that a break was called so that I could attempt to regain some composure.

During the break my lawyer only asked me one question: "What does your sister have against you?"

"She's *not* my sister!" I blurted.

"Well, if you want to perjure yourself, that's up to you. And for heaven's sake, can you stop your crying!" He left and went to sit with Clarence's lawyer. They appeared to be sharing a joke.

At the end of the hearing, the Judge gave his ruling. He said, "While Mr. Baird may not have been the most glamorous of husbands, he has been a good provider," and concluded, "The children will stay where they are."

I would be awarded $10,000 as my part of the settlement although Clarence and I owned a 100-acre home with a 25' by 50' swimming pool, two vehicles, cattle, and farm equipment, and had a total debt of only $6,000. I retained joint ownership of the house. I later signed my interest in the house over to Clarence because I felt that if the girls were to be brought up in this house, I did not want to impose any undue hardship on them. I would only have infrequent visiting privileges with the girls. I felt dead and wished that I was.

Leaving the courtroom, Carmen proceeded to get in an elevator with Clarence. I called to her and asked if I could speak to her a minute.

I told her: "I hope I never see you again, and in case I don't, I want you to know that you are not my sister." I had never told her before what my father had told me. He was quite sure that Carmen was not his daughter. Now I wanted her to know.

I returned to Cape Breton, to my life with Larry. In tears most days, I managed somehow to keep working. I thought many times about suicide. What stopped me was telling myself that someday the children might need me and I wouldn't be there for them.

I was going to be able to have the children at Christmas and so flew to Halifax to bring them back with me for the first Christmas we would spend together in some time. Larry and I bought them gifts of pyjamas, dolls and each a new long coat. It was wonderful to see them happy and laughing again. I felt alive again, but the time came much too soon for me to take them to the airport. This didn't seem right, and watching them walk to the plane broke my heart again in many pieces. It was killing me emotionally.

I later learned from the girls that their father had taken all their gifts from us and thrown them into the stove.

Attempts to see them more often were unsuccessful and I was met with resistance and hostility any time I tried. I decided to go to another lawyer to attempt to get visiting rights expanded and clarified; they were. However, Clarence and his mother played defence and kept me away so my efforts were futile.

Our divorce was final in 1976, and in 1977 Clarence married Barbara Wilmott. She moved in to become stepmother to my girls. I was told by Clarence to stay away from the house and to stop writing letters to my daughters.

I felt like I had nothing left; no children, no family, no friends, no self-confidence, no self-respect and no self-worth. The only person in my life at all was Larry, with the good, and the bad.

Chapter Eight

What Manner of Man is This?

L arry and I were married in March of 1977 at the Glace Bay Miner's Museum. It was a pretty wedding in an old-fashioned setting with oil lamps and candles lit. Larry's brother walked me down the aisle and whispered, "You look beautiful." Larry looked as handsome as I had ever seen him, dressed in his tuxedo, and my stomach was filled with butterflies. He smiled, and my heart melted. We were pronounced "husband and wife."

We were enjoying the reception and our guests when I was distracted by Larry flirting openly with the waitresses. They were being charmed by him as I had been. Realizing that he had been drinking a little too much, I suggested to him that it was time to leave, "Larry, dear, I am really anxious to leave now so we can be together alone."

"Oh sure, I know what you want now, don't I, hmmmmmm?" And he grabbed my behind and winked. I was embarrassed that guests might have heard and seen, but I just smiled and said nothing.

I hurriedly guided him out and into our car. He was still carrying a drink in his hand. We had planned to spend our wedding night at a hotel, but realizing he was in no condition to go anywhere, I drove us home. I helped Larry get undressed and put him into bed. Within minutes he had fallen asleep. Such was our honeymoon.

A better job opportunity had become available for me and I was now employed with Atomic Energy as an Accounts Payable clerk. Larry had also applied for a position with the same Company and was ecstatic when he was hired as a Planner. No longer would he have to sell vacuum cleaners. I knew he had found that job degrading and was so happy that he had found more meaningful work at last. He never talked about wanting to pursue a career in the ministry and in fact seldom even made any references to the church or his faith. It seemed that his spiritual self had all but disappeared. When I prayed, he discouraged me by saying, "Forget it, that won't do you any good." This, from a former minister of the Church, a man who I had believed was so spiritual! I couldn't believe what I was hearing him say. I didn't want to believe it! I had to hold on to my faith, in spite of him.

We were still having a difficult time financially, so when I saw an ad in the local paper looking for a couple to live-in and manage the Champlain Motel in exchange for free accommodation, I applied. They required someone who could speak French. The owner was from Ste. Pierre Miquelon and a large part of his business was meeting people at the airport who were traveling back and forth to

France. Learning French as a child was going to be an asset, and I was hired.

While packing to move to our new accommodation I decided to check the basement of our old house to be sure we were not leaving anything behind. I had not gone to the basement for some time and was not prepared for what I found there. In one corner there was a display of dozens of magazines, opened and placed side by side. They were pornographic magazines. Pictures of naked women were lined up. Garbage bags were on the floor and contained more magazines—many more. I now realized why Larry had been in the basement when I had come downstairs in the night unexpectedly. I confronted him and he admitted he had been "enjoying himself." I had been so naïve and inexperienced about sex and found this situation difficult to accept. Was this normal? I didn't think so.

Larry and I moved into an apartment upstairs from the motel office, with free rent. We arrived home at 4:30 p.m. to go on duty at the motel. We greeted guests and registered them. My other duties included delivering towels to their rooms, address any complaints and drive back and forth to the airport to provide them with transportation. There was no restaurant at the motel and I was asked to prepare and deliver breakfast to those wanting it. I managed to do this before leaving for work. Breakfast requests turned into breakfast and late dinner requests. Our living room became a dining room where I served dinner. I was wearing out and Larry was not contributing to the workload. I began to refuse providing any meals. One day I overheard the owner discussing me with a friend: "They get free rent and she don't want to do nothing." I was livid and told him so. We left the motel and found a bungalow to rent in a place called Marion Bridge.

Our finances were even more strained now that we had to pay rent, and we talked about moving out West. If I was not going to be able to see my children, then maybe Larry at least would be able to see his. We sold whatever furnishings we owned and with the $10,000. I had received as a divorce settlement, traded Larry's car for a camper truck and bought a U-Haul to transport our personal possessions and the large electronic organ.

We arrived in Calgary and parked in a campsite. Our first priority was to find work but when asked "What is your address?" we had none other than the campsite. If we looked for accommodation first, they would ask, "Where do you work?" We went to the Unemployment Insurance Office to apply for benefits. While we were there, a recruiter from Fort McMurray was interviewing for positions with Syncrude Canada Ltd. Larry was interviewed and told that he would be contacted if they had a position for him.

When I met with a counselor at the Unemployment office, I was asked if I would be interested in a position with them. Within a few days I was interviewed and hired. I had started my first day's work when I received a phone call from Larry. He had been offered a position as a Planner in Fort McMurray and we needed to move right away. My first day with the Unemployment Insurance office was also my last!

We were to be provided with free accommodation for one month in a fully furnished trailer and we were eligible to receive a grant of $32,000 towards the purchase of a new home. Larry's salary would be more than adequate and he would start work right away.

We left the campgrounds in Calgary and drove North on a very narrow road to Fort McMurray. There was a distinct lack of the lush vegetation I was accustomed to seeing. The trees were sparse and thin, and here and there I noticed an old abandoned vehicle by the roadside. No flowers, no people, no houses could be seen anywhere. It was desolate country, and it seemed we were getting farther away from civilization. Finally we did arrive at a service station in a place called Wandering River. There was nothing more there than a gas pump and a very small restaurant. We filled the gas tank and continued on our journey north. About two hours later we arrived in Marianna Lakes, another place with a gas pump and restaurant.

We finally arrived in Fort McMurray. They had said it was a "booming town." Everywhere there was construction; malls were being built, apartment complexes and houses were being erected, and roads were being paved.

We located our trailer easily, and I was pleasantly surprised to see that it was fully furnished with everything we would require, even dishes, pots and pans, and towels. They hadn't forgotten a single thing and we finally had a place where we could live comfortably, at least for a little while, until we could afford a more permanent home. Things were looking up and Larry and I were feeling more cheerful than we had for some time. We had come through some very dark days, but we were still together. We had each other and we would try to build a better future. It did seem possible now. The saying goes, "Money Can't Buy Happiness," but we knew that not having enough to buy even the basics, could certainly make it difficult, and it had. It had taken its toll on our relationship.

Larry's job with Syncrude had given him a more positive outlook on life. He seemed renewed with energy and his spirit was lifted as mine was. I was seeing the "old Larry" again; this was the same man I had fallen in love with! Our lovemaking increased in frequency and intensity and Larry was once again telling me how much he loved me. But did he? I wondered. Yet I hoped.

I decided I wanted to do more than stay at home, and visited Syncrude's employment office. It seemed there were many jobs available with the Company and I applied for an "Accounts Payable Clerk" position. Within a few days, I was contacted for an interview and was hired. I could now travel to work with Larry each day. We would have two salaries now, and be in a position to look for permanent accommodation.

With the $32,000 interest-free loan that Syncrude offered to all of their employees at that time, we were able to purchase a brand new home. We had come so far since the tiny trailer in Glace Bay. We should be happy now, but without my children, complete happiness to me was a thing of the past. There was always an emptiness that couldn't be filled.

We first met Klara when we went to her beauty parlour. She was tall, blonde and buxom, with a strong German accent. She seemed very friendly and especially seemed to like Larry. As she fussed over his hair they joked and laughed. It was obvious she was impressed with his charm and he with hers. I was experiencing pangs of jealousy but had no idea at that time that Klara would figure prominently in his future.

Syncrude was doing a great deal to assist women employees with their career development. I was enjoying my work but soon realized that in order to be promoted beyond the Administrative level, I would need to finish my degree. Syncrude would pay for all my courses after I had completed them successfully.

Living in Fort McMurray meant living in the dark most of the winter, and in daylight for most of the summer. It was a booming town, the salaries were high and most of the time so were a great many of the people! Shopping carts were the norm in the liquor store. It was a town "way up north" and there was only one highway out. The closest city was Edmonton about a five-hour drive south. Going further north meant ending up in the native community of Fort Chipewan, and we never went north on the highway.

There didn't seem to be any extended families in Fort McMurray and the average age was the mid-twenties. The place was overrun with bars and that was the main activity there. We both drank frequently now; often more than we should. It was a way of life and it was a way to forget. Drinking seemed to numb the pain of being without my children, if only temporarily. Inhibitions lowered and Larry and I were fighting constantly. He seemed to be able to set me off for no reason at all, or so it seemed.

One day Larry came up behind me and stood there. "Your neck is dirty," he said.

"What?" I said, surprised that my neck would be dirty. Cleanliness had always been important to me and I hadn't been anywhere to get dirty.

"Your neck is dirty," he said again.

"Well, I guess I'll have to wash it." I went into the bathroom and started to wash but I could not see any dirt on the facecloth. What was he talking about? Why was he saying that?

He had also been telling me that my breath was bad; he told me this so often that I began to question myself about it. I brushed vigorously and used more mouthwash than usual. I was convinced my breath was not bad.

I arrived home one day to find new clothes laid out on the bed. Larry had bought me a new outfit.

"How thoughtful!" I said. It was a straight skirt, a pullover sweater and a padded bra. He wanted me to try them on, which I proceeded to do. The skirt was tight and clung in places that showed my curves. I had never worn a padded bra before, but put it on to please Larry and then pulled the sweater over my head. It clung tightly to accentuate the padded bra.

I much preferred sweaters to be loose but Larry looked at me and said, "Now there! That's how I want you to dress. You look sexy."

I didn't mind looking sexy in the privacy of our home, but these were clothes that he expected me to wear out in public. In public!

"Thank you, Larry," I said, but I planned to hide these clothes away, including the padded bra. I didn't want to wear them outside of the house.

"And just because you look so sexy, I'm taking you out for the evening." Larry stunned me! In spite of my excuses, he insisted. I was doomed! I didn't want other men looking at me "that way".

"Where are we going, Larry?" I asked.

"It's a surprise!"

I reached for my coat, but he insisted I didn't need it. I put it on anyway. I wanted to cover up. Larry drove downtown trying to be amorous all the way there, and then stopped the car in front of a bar.

"Let's go inside for a quick drink before dinner. I hear there is entertainment!" He seemed to be excited about the entertainment and hurried me inside. It was dark inside the bar and loud music was playing as he found a place to sit, close to the stage.

He had just ordered our drinks when the entertainment was announced. "Lonely Little Lulu" entered wearing a school uniform. I thought it looked very much like the uniform I had worn when I was taught by the Sisters of Charity. She was holding a big sucker and I assumed she must be a comedy act, but she said nothing. She began to dance provocatively to the music and with one swift pull she removed her uniform to reveal a red bikini. Larry applauded loudly and she danced near the edge of the stage. This was not the kind of "entertainment" I had expected. We were at a "strip club" and she was an exotic dancer.

"Larry, I want to leave." I rose from my seat but he reached for my hand. "Sit down!" he said firmly. Not wanting to create a scene, I did what I was told. But I resolved that he would never put me in a situation like this again—ever!

What was he trying to turn me into? Was he trying to change me?

I began to realize Larry's actions were his way of destroying my self-confidence. Once my self-confidence was destroyed, then it would be easy for him to control me. I could only wonder what he wanted to do with me.

Who was this man I was now married to? Had he lost his vision as a Christian and a preacher? My mind went back to how I had admired him and felt about him in the days when I first went to church and listened to him preach. Had that all been an act?

I told Larry I wanted to start going to church again. "We both need to go back to church, Larry. Our marriage is falling apart." Somewhat reluctantly, he finally agreed.

We began attending a Baptist Church each Sunday. People were interested to know all about us but I still wouldn't trust anyone enough to talk about our past and could never admit the pride I felt about my children. I couldn't talk about them to anyone and felt I was living a lie.

Soon Larry had charmed his way into preaching at the church when the minister was away. I no longer believed a word he said from the pulpit but was enjoying the fellowship with the church members. They were impressed with his sermons, as I had once been. They thought he was such a warm, caring individual and Christian, just as I had once believed. I knew differently now. He was deceiving them as I was, by not telling them the difference. But how could I?

I knew that Larry was still spending time with pornographic materials; I had seen them. I did not approve and told him so. He would only laugh and say, "What a prude you are!"

Nor did I like the way he talked to me; it made me feel cheap. "Come here baby; show me what you've got!" and "Look what I've got"—waving his privates at me. "Want to watch a porn video with me? You'd love it." And when I declined: "Oh, never mind, I'll watch it myself then. It'll be more fun without you."

As I was undressing one night for bed, he snapped my picture.

"Larry, what are doing? Give me that camera!"

As he ran, I threatened him: "Don't you ever dare develop that film!"

I checked the camera as soon as I got the chance but the film was gone. When I asked him about it he laughed it off, saying he had destroyed it. I highly doubted he had, but had no way of ever knowing for sure.

Another argument had started and Larry kept taunting me. I hated to fight, I hated it! I wanted to have some peace and quiet, but still he ranted at me. Finally, I could take it no longer and started to scream. My screaming got louder but it seemed that the screaming was coming from somewhere else, somewhere in the distance, outside of myself. I placed my hands over my ears to stop the noise, but I could still hear the screaming. Finally it stopped. I realized the screaming I had heard was my own. Larry was being silent. He must have realized he had pushed me as far as he could—at least, for the time being.

Our finances were greatly improved, so we decided to make a trip to Edmonton and spend a couple of nights at a motel and enjoy the city. We had been out for the evening and were returning to our room when a party being held in another room attracted Larry. He wanted to join and did so. I was tired and my feet were hurting so I went back to our room, took my shoes off and waited for Larry.

Within a short time he entered and brought with him two young men. I had no idea what he had planned.

He began to brag to the men about me: "Isn't she beautiful?"

One of them came over to where I was sitting and put his hand on my leg. He proceeded to try and kiss me.

I was taken aback. "Larry, stop him!"

Larry appeared to be enjoying the scene and made no effort to come over to me. He pulled his shirt outside of his slacks and put one foot on the bed to watch whatever this other man was up to.

"Larry?" I jumped to my feet and ran as fast as I could out the door and into an elevator. The elevator door was still open when Larry jumped in. He said nothing.

"Don't you dare come near me! Stay away from me!" I had pressed the button for the main floor. I got off quickly in the lobby and Larry remained in the elevator. I didn't know what to do.

I sat in the Lobby for what seemed like hours when one of the men who had been in our room came to sit with me. He had not approached me in the room and was being sympathetic to my situation.

"I'm not married," he said, "but if I was, I would hope my wife would be just like you." He smiled. "Larry wants you to go back upstairs. I'll go with you to make sure that the other fellow is gone, and give you my room number if you get frightened again."

I did not want to cause a scene in the hotel. I had been scared to death but now I was angry and I was not afraid of anything. I knew that if Larry tried to lay a hand on me he would be sorry. I felt hurt, but I felt strong. I returned to the room and went to bed.

What kind of a man was this that I was married to now? Yet I felt that I needed to hold on and do whatever I could to make this marriage work. I had failed once at marriage and I could not do it again.

I was doing well at work and getting promotions. Work was fine but home was hell.

Chapter Nine

The Furnace of Affliction

I was lying in bed one morning when Larry came into the room, got on the bed and suddenly straddled me, put his hands around my throat and started to choke me. I started to scream and he freed one hand to reach out and close the window. The choking was getting tighter and I was gasping, pleading with him to stop; reminding him of his boys, anything I thought would bring him to his senses. Through the panic I thought, "So this is how I'm going to die." From somewhere deep within me came a blood-curdling scream. Either I found the strength to push him off me or the scream startled him, and I was able to get away and run downstairs. I was hyperventilating and I wrapped my arms around an end table. Larry appeared frightened and asked if he should call a doctor. I said no.

After the hyperventilating stopped I felt like I could kill anything that got in my way and that included Larry. He knew better than to come near me.

The next day I saw the Employee Counsellor at work and told him what had happened.

"You don't have to go home, but if you decide to I want you to tell Larry that you have spoken to me and told me everything."

I did so and also told Larry that I was leaving him and not ever to come near me again.

Failing at a second marriage or not, I *was* leaving. "For better or worse" did not include this. I quickly found accommodation in Syncrude's apartments and arranged to move.

I was now in a different financial position with only one salary to live on. A career opportunity arose in Edmonton. I was interviewed for the position and hired. With a promotion and salary increase, I moved to the city and found an apartment.

Larry continued to phone me. "I miss you, Laura. Please come back home. I love you!"

Words, just words, I thought.

"I cannot understand how you could do the things you have done to me if you love me. As a matter of fact, I can't believe the things you have done, even if you didn't love me. You have moved so far from being the man I once knew and loved. What has happened to you?"

"But I'm still the same person, Laura. I never meant to harm you. I don't know why I behaved as I did. Maybe the devil made me do it. He does tempt us Christians, you know. I will do whatever you say, just let me come and get you. Or at least let me come and talk to you. I know we can sort this all out. I want to make our marriage work!"

"I don't know, I'll think about it." But I wasn't feeling confident that I ever wanted to see him again.

I contacted a minister in the city and asked him to meet with the two of us at my apartment. I could not bring myself to tell him about the intimate details of our relationship and the minister tried to persuade me to try to mend our differences.

In spite of my resistance, Larry had charmed me once again. I wanted to believe he was sincere about changing and making our marriage work. Maybe I had been somewhat to blame, I thought. I would give us another chance. So again I returned to Fort McMurray.

Larry and I bought a new home in a lovely area of the town. We would start again. I had to be both crazy and blind to believe that things would change.

When I returned to Syncrude the position I had left was no longer available, but I was given the opportunity to join the Training Department. They had a new program where selected individuals who had been Supervisors would be sent for a year to their Training Department in order to become "better supervisors".

One of the trainers was Cindy and we became very close friends. We would become life-long friends and confided in each other about everything. It was great to have someone that I could talk to freely.

I was provided the opportunity to take courses in Human Resources in Maine, Florida, and Colorado, traveling to places I had never been before and doing things I had never done. I had the chance to go up in a Hot Air balloon in

Aspen, Colorado and it was thrilling to be so far up in the sky. Somehow it made me feel closer to heaven.

I became a licensed Kepner-Tregoe Instructor, teaching their Decision Analysis, Potential Problem Analysis, Problem Analysis, and Situational Appraisal processes, and I was a certified Myers-Briggs teacher. I began to teach Syncrude Employees Performance Appraisal Systems, Planning, Supervisory Skills, Effective Presentations, and all the other programs offered by Syncrude. I became one of the coaches for their Management Program and flew to Banff and Jasper for their one-week Team Skills programs. I was gaining such valuable work experience and I was receiving promotions. I was gaining a great deal in resilience and self-confidence: the furnace of life was improving my mettle!

One of the classes I took was "Forced Writing". In one of the exercises, we were to start writing when they gave the word "GO"; we were to write as fast as our hand could possibly move, without thinking, without stopping. We were to continue constantly until they finally said "STOP!" We were given a title only, which was "Where do you think you are in your life?" The exercise lasted for exactly fourteen minutes during which time the only thing the coach said was "Keep on writing, keep on writing" over and over. At the end of those fourteen minutes I was shaking. I stopped and read what I had written. I could not believe it! I carried it with me and read it many times over.

WHERE DO YOU THINK YOU ARE IN YOUR LIFE?

Keep on fighting, keep on fighting

Win, not fail... Struggle, not stop... Gain, not lose

Free to be me…An individual…

Not looking back…but Forward…Forward

Quit?... Not me…for to be free

Is a God-given gift of Life.

Why stop to brood? Get in the mood

For all that's bright and new

Be still, my soul

I know the good, the true, the strong

Past fights still push me ever on

To win anew…and still belong

To all the friends I trust…I'll be

A spirit of eternity

To be more than a friend could ask

To fight and strive to do a task

To be a best of everything

I hope…I win…I try…I ask

Are these the thoughts of one I know?

Could God be watching me below?

Does He still care? Does He still dare

To use my gifts and help me share?

I know He does…I feel His love

And when I look around this world

I thank God this life's my pearl

Whoever stops to think may trip

Whoever trips may stumble down

This is not up…I'll look away

I'll try to see another day

For who is there…I should be true?

To you…To all…and yes, I do

Believe I know my life

I feel I've lived and loved through strife

How can the free not stop and say

I'll be a bird…To life eternal

On the brink of greater things…Than man has made.

One day a letter arrived in the mail addressed to Mr. & Mrs. Larry Boone. Since my name was also on the envelope, I opened it and a photo fell out. I picked it up and saw to my horror that it was a photo of me taken while Larry and I had been camping near a beach. I had been wearing a T-shirt and someone had circled my breasts and written across the photo, "Laura".

The letter was from a couple to whom Larry had sent the photo, and they were returning it. The letter thanked Larry for the picture and said they were very interested in getting together for a "swinging session". Larry had obtained their name from a Swinger's magazine and had replied. I was horrified. If he wrote to them and sent my photo, how many others had he written or sent my photo to? Would I be recognized by those people?

I confronted Larry about the letter and his reply was, "The only reason I married you was because I thought you were good swapping material." That was the nail in the coffin of our marriage! No more! I had had enough and was leaving, this time forever. And I did. As I was packing the soft side of me took over and I thought, "Larry is ten years older than I am, so he will have a shorter time to get back on his feet." Looking back, why should I have cared? But I took very little of the furnishings and left our Grand Marquis car for Larry.

Chapter Ten

A New Beginning

I moved into a condominium and the only furniture I had was a small bed and a table with one chair. I set about trying to make this my home. Cardboard boxes turned upside down and covered with a tablecloth made fine tables; lawn chairs covered with afghans were my living room furniture. I was moving ahead with my life, and on my own again.

Every year I used my vacation time to travel back to Nova Scotia to try and see my daughters. One year I rented a cottage at Mountain Gap Inn so that the girls and I could spend some time together. I had phoned to tell Clarence when I would arrive, and that I would like to have the girls with me at the cottage for a few days at least.

Clarence's wife Barbara arrived with my daughters. As they ran to greet me Barbara stopped them and said, "Clarence and I are going to Halifax and the girls are going with us. They don't love you anyway."

"If it makes you feel better to say that," I said with a sinking heart. I didn't know what else to say, but the insult had taken me aback.

"But Mommy, I do love you!" Julie was saying as she ran to me to hold me tight.

"Me too, and I want to stay here!" Elizabeth was right behind her.

Barbara was holding Lisa's hand as she broke away from her and came to join her sisters. "Please can't we stay?"

"No!" Barbara shouted. "Now get in the car—we're leaving!"

"Don't upset them. Just leave them for a little while. Can't you see that they want to be with me?" I was pleading. It just wasn't right of her and Clarence to do this to us.

Barbara walked over to the girls and gave them a push towards the car. I wanted to push her back, I wanted to grab her and shake her. I had done nothing to her, so why was she acting this way? I didn't want to upset the girls any further so hugged them and said that I loved them and that I would still be here when they returned from Halifax and would see them then.

They seemed reassured, and turned to give me a hug before they left.

Some years were more successful than others but through it all, my daughters and I remained in touch and were able to rebuild our bond with one another. Each year I sent gifts for every occasion and learned much later that they were never allowed to open their Christmas gifts from me until *after* Christmas.

I also learned that Clarence had thrown away anything I had left behind including my birth certificate and my special shoes from the Rehabilitation Centre. The worst loss was when I found out that he had also sold my dear Grammy Lil's piano; it had been so special to me and now I would never see or play it again.

My mother was now living in a Senior Citizen's apartment and I visited her on my trips back to Nova Scotia. I had never confided in her about any of my problems but she phoned me frequently in Fort McMurray to complain about hers.

I sent her $200.00 a month for years but that was never enough. She wanted me to buy all her clothes and send them from Fort McMurray. Once I sent her a box with about $500.00 worth of things only to have her phone me within a couple of weeks.

"Nothing fits me! And I can't return them. I had the blouses altered but they made the sleeves too short. The coat is way too big and it looks like hell on me."

"What about the housecoat and the slacks?"

"They don't fit me either. And who did you think would wear those colours anyway?"

"I thought they were lovely."

"Lovely? Maybe that's your style, but not mine. Your taste is in your mouth!" She almost spat out the words.

She wanted me to send her more. As usual, no matter what I did, nothing pleased her. But she was my mother and she had no one else except her sister Margaret.

Aunt Margaret by now had also moved into the same Senior Citizen's apartments and she was constantly in tears over my mother. She gave Mom whatever she asked for including financial support; but that was never enough to please her. Mom continually ranted and raved until Aunt Margaret became ill. Her daughter finally moved her to Ontario.

Except for me, my mother was now completely alone. My sister Carmen had long ago decided to break all contact with her and it had been many years since they had seen one another.

They spoke harshly about each other.

In 1982, Elizabeth, now sixteen years old, was the first of my daughters to take me up on an offer of a free ticket to Fort McMurray anytime she or the other girls wanted one. Elizabeth was always the one with a mind of her own, and a strong determination. It was wonderful being able to spend time with her in my own place. It was New Year's and we celebrated.

I was still having difficulty with walking and decided to see a Specialist in Edmonton. I had hoped to get a prescription for proper shoes but the Specialist felt there was a good chance that surgery on my right foot could straighten it. Surgery was booked and the bones in my right foot were totally rebuilt and the tension cord released. It would allow me for the first time to walk on the bottom of the foot rather than on the side.

I was in a cast and on crutches and lived alone. I was now living in a condominium with an upstairs bedroom. Each morning I would manage to get out of bed and with the aid of my crutches get to the bathroom to bathe and dress. I would go downstairs on my behind, one step at a time and at night would return upstairs by sitting on the steps and going backwards one step at a time.

I was only out of the hospital for two weeks before I decided I should go back to work. And so I managed with crutches to hop on the employee bus. I soon discovered that most people were not sympathetic enough to give me their seat. The exception was a mentally challenged young man named Randy who would get on the bus early enough to get the front seat; he would then give it to me when I boarded. He was kinder than the others. I resolved to drive my car with a walking cast and put my crutches into the back seat.

Shopping for groceries was a challenge but I managed somehow. Many times when I tried to enter building doors, people would not hold them open for me but let them close in my face. The cast remained on for three months before I had it removed. I had to learn to walk all over again. I had never been able to walk on the sole of my right foot and it was extremely sensitive. Gradually I moved from crutches to a cane. A mold of my right foot had been made in order to build new shoes.

In 1983 I obtained a divorce from Larry on the grounds of his adultery; he had been living with another woman. Before long he married the hairdresser Klara—their engagement was in the paper before the divorce became final. And so they would live happily ever after—or not. Prior to re-marrying, Larry had seen me at work and asked me if I would consider marrying him again. My reply was decisive: "Not in a million years!" He told me he was marrying Klara "for her money".

We still both worked for the same Company and could not avoid seeing each other frequently. He would keep me posted about their arguments and how she had threatened to commit suicide. Apparently encouraging her to do so, he had handed her a gun. How I had misread and misjudged this man to whom I used to listen, so ardently, when he was my church minister! It's true, I suppose, that you cannot judge a book by its cover.

I was stopping, on one occasion, in Montreal airport on my way back to Fort McMurray and had contacted my father who was living in Quebec. His wife Charlotte was in Nova Scotia at the time so he said he would be able to meet me. We had a brief visit and it was the first and only time I remember him saying "I love you, Laura".

In 1984 Julie was twenty years old when she came to Fort McMurray. I had booked a trip to Las Vegas for the two of us. We stayed at the Flamingo Hilton Hotel and it was an exciting time. We went to "Circus Circus" and she won a huge stuffed dog that she named "Hilton". Hilton was required to ride in cargo and she worried about him being all by himself. I had been so happy to have her with me and now I had to see her leave again.

Being single in Fort McMurray meant there were always lots of things to do. When I wasn't working, I was partying, dancing, and drinking. There were many single men and I was asked out on dates frequently. One evening I had invited someone to dinner and was drinking while preparing the meal. He arrived and we drank wine with our meal, and then had liqueurs with our coffee. He thought he was going to stay the night but I did not want him to. Instead of telling

119

him to get a taxi I stupidly offered to drive him home—a decision I would regret!

On the way, there was a Police "check-stop" and they pulled all the cars over to the side. When my car was approached, the police officer asked me to step outside. When he asked me to walk the straight line I tried to explain to him that I could not due to polio and having a limp.

"Could you give me a different sobriety test please?" I had asked politely but he ignored me.

I tried to walk straight but as usual my limp threw me off balance. I failed the test. I was taken to the police station and given a Breathalyzer and I was found to be over the legal limit. I was impaired. I was allowed to go home with a driver and told to return the next day for fingerprinting. This was it! I was now a criminal! I had never been inside a jail ever and it was totally humiliating.

I was to go to court and I obtained a lawyer. The police officer had not "read me my rights" and so the lawyer said there was a chance I would not be charged. I could not drive until the court date.

I attended court to face my humiliation. The police officer testified that he had read me my rights. I was called to the stand and had memories of the last time I had been in a courtroom.

At the end of the hearing the judge said, "Even though I find Laura Boone to be very credible, she was drinking and the police officer wasn't; therefore I must take the police officer's word." I was fined $400.00, and given a 6-month suspension of license. My name appeared in the newspaper in bold letters for all to see. I felt I had gone as low as I could and whatever self-worth I had managed to hold on to, was completely gone now.

The impaired charge did however cause me to think about what drinking was doing to me. I decided that if I was an alcoholic, I had better find out before something worse happened. It was a difficult and humiliating thing to do, but I dialed the number for Alcoholics Anonymous. They said someone would pick me up to take me to their regular meeting. I went and felt both scared, and humbled. One by one each AA member stood and said their first name, and I was encouraged to tell my story; how alcohol had affected me. I was made to feel like I was welcome and I realized that I was not alone.

I was still not convinced that I was an alcoholic but determined to find out for myself before I went back to an AA meeting. I would not drink; and I didn't. Then I would take one drink and stop—and I could. If I could stop, then I would manage without AA and never have to admit that I could be an alcoholic. I now was able to have a social drink and always stopped after no more than two. I never drove if I had a drink. I had stooped as low as I was prepared to go for alcohol.

Chapter Eleven

Saying Goodbye

In 1985 Lisa came to Fort McMurray to spend some time with me. She was twenty-two now and was a nurse. I was so happy finally to be able to have her with me. I knew that I wanted to be closer to her and to Julie and Elizabeth. They were the most precious people in my whole life and I needed to be able to see them more often.

Lisa had previously suggested that she would like me to renew my relationship with Carmen. She knew only that Carmen and I had not been speaking but had no idea why, nor what Carmen had said in court when she was a witness for Clarence. In spite of the hard feelings I still harboured, and the lack of trust because of it, I would do anything Lisa asked me to do. As a first attempt at reconciliation, I sent Carmen and David a Christmas card with a note. It said, "Let bygones be bygones and although I cannot forget, I can forgive." I received a card from Carmen in response to mine but there was no message with it. It was simply signed: "Carmen and David."

On a trip to Ontario I phoned Carmen to suggest we meet at the airport. Carmen and David were there to greet me. It was a start.

I was in my forties when I learned to smoke cigarettes. It was my crutch and companion after that. Whenever I was alone and feeling sad (as I often did), I would smoke. For years everyone around me smoked, yet I didn't. Now it was becoming unpopular and I had started. Was it the rebel in me showing itself? I would live to regret my smoking habit.

In 1986 I returned from a visit to Nova Scotia and heard the startling news. There had been a boating accident on the Athabasca River, and Larry was missing and presumed drowned! He had fallen overboard without a life jacket when the group attempted to go through the rapids.

Larry's boss arrived at my desk and passed me a photo of myself that he had found in Larry's desk. He looked at me sadly and said, "I thought you should have it."

Why had Larry kept a photo of me in his desk? For a moment I allowed myself to think that maybe he had still loved me.

Larry's body was found two weeks later on the banks of an Indian village.

How ironic, I thought, that Larry had once told me he was marrying Klara "for her money" and now his insurance money had made her even richer.

In 1987 I completed my degree and graduated from Athabasca University in Edmonton. With a degree, I was now eligible for more promotions with Syncrude and was soon put in charge of their Management Development Program.

Everything was going well in my career, I owned a new home and I was financially secure. But something was missing in my life. What more could I want? I knew what I needed to be happy but I was not going to find it in Fort McMurray, so far away from my children. They were growing up and I wanted to be part of their lives; their weddings, their children. So I made a decision that I was going to move back to Nova Scotia. I was able to sell my house quickly and left my job with Syncrude after eleven years with the Company. I could hardly wait to return to my home province.

Chapter Twelve

Home Again

I was happy to be back in Nova Scotia. So many times I had missed and longed for the smell of salt water, and the familiar surroundings. I was home and I was never going to leave again!

Soon I was settled into an apartment in Halifax and started looking for work. Within a few weeks I was contacted to be interviewed for a position as Personnel Manager with the Provincial Government. I had no idea what a Personnel Manager did but was determined to convince the interview panel that I was qualified. The day of the interview arrived and I had dressed in my best "Personnel Manager" suit. "First impressions are important," I decided. I had taught "Interviewing Skills" with Syncrude, so was confident I knew what to expect.

As I entered the interview room I was introduced to the panel that would be assessing my qualifications. Two members of the panel were Deputy Ministers and the position would require me to report to them. It might have been intimidating being interviewed by such high level individuals had I not been part of Syncrude's Management and dealt with Senior Management on a regular basis. I was ready for their questions and thought, 'Fire Away!'

"You will be responsible for staff of two government departments," they told me, after informing me that the job was mine.

Elizabeth came home from University in Ottawa and brought with her a gift bag for me from Carmen. It was several bottles of high-priced perfumes.

Then, several months later, Carmen visited me at my apartment. She and I had re-connected after all these years and I had made amends as Lisa had asked me to.

I continued to work and was promoted to Director of Personnel. I rented a Cape Cod house on Capri Island in Porter's Lake with the intention of buying it. My mother entered my life again when she phoned and wanted to come and live with me. I moved her in with me and almost immediately she found fault with the house and the location and wanted to move again. So I signed a one-year lease on a large apartment and we moved to the city. I took my vacation to get everything unpacked and get her settled. Each day I lifted her into the bathtub, lifted her out, dried her off and then did her hair. Every morning I prepared her breakfast and lunch and made sure she had what she needed before I left for work.

Within two weeks she started to say, "I shouldn't have moved here," and, "You don't even want me here!" I asked her what I could do that I wasn't doing or what I was doing that I shouldn't. She would just stick her chin in the air. Now she wanted me to help her find somewhere else to live. I refused. I was totally exasperated with her foolishness. I had just signed a one-year lease on a place that I could not afford nor would have taken if she had not wanted to move. She proceeded to get on the phone to an acquaintance and said, "You wouldn't believe how she is treating me—I have to get out of here, and will you come and get me?"

I had had enough and told her that when I returned from work the next day she had better be gone. She was.

I soon heard from others that she was now boarding in a place in Bear River where they took seniors to live. This was her choice and I had nothing to say.

Chapter Thirteen

"Here's Hoping!"

In December 1991 I went to Ottawa to spend Christmas with my sister Carmen and her husband David. They invited a friend of theirs, Mark Warren, over for the evening. Mark was a widower with two daughters, Christine, 20, and Lea, 17. He was 54 years old.

Mark was a tall, dark, and handsome man and seemed so mannerly and well-spoken. I was immediately attracted to his personality and his sense of humor. Mark had spent twenty-six years in the army and was then working for the federal government as a Senior Investigator. He invited me to his home for dinner and to meet his daughters. They were beautiful girls, big and tall. I impressed them all by offering to make an apple pie for dessert, using a wine bottle for a rolling pin since they didn't seem to have one.

The week I had in Ottawa came to an end far too quickly and Mark took me to the airport. We agreed to correspond. His mother lived in Halifax and he planned to visit there soon, so we would see each other again.

In the summer of 1992 Mark arrived in Halifax for a visit. He took me to meet his mother and we immediately liked each other. She lived in an apartment and spent her time watching TV, reading, and smoking cigarettes. I was impressed with how spotless she kept everything. She was so happy that Mark and I were seeing each other.

Mark returned home and it was going to be a longer time before we could get together again. We kept in touch through many phone calls and letters but we were lonely without each other. Trying to maintain a long distance romance was not easy.

The summer of 1993 arrived and so did Mark. This time, although we were happy to see each other, the relationship was more difficult. My daughter Lisa and her young baby were living with me and I seemed to have other priorities.

And so, all too quickly Mark had to return to Ottawa. Although we still kept in touch occasionally, we drifted apart and he began to pursue other relationships, as did I. However, neither of us seemed to find what we were looking for in anyone else.

An employee in my Department approached me to ask if I was related to a Victor Gidney. I had taken my maiden name again after my divorce from Larry, and was known as Laura Gidney.

"Why, yes, I am. He's my father. Why do you ask?"

"My uncle is in the Rehabilitation Centre and I was visiting him there when he introduced me to his room-mate Victor Gidney. Mr. Gidney is not able to speak now."

I thanked him for the information and decided to visit my father at the Centre. I brought paper and pencil thinking that we may be able to communicate in some fashion if he was unable to speak. When I arrived in his room, he was in a wheelchair and although much older than I remembered him, he was still a handsome man. He looked as though he recognized me and broke into a big smile. I passed him the notepaper and pencil I had brought and he took it eagerly and began to try and write something. He showed me the paper excitedly and he had drawn a huge letter "L" and then an even larger letter "V" outside of it. I believed that he was saying that he knew I was Laura and his name was Victor. I had also brought photos of his grandchildren and great-grandchildren, which he gazed at. His eyes became watery; then he quickly took one of the photos and, as if to hide it, shoved it underneath his belt. I wondered if he was hiding it from Charlotte. I pushed his wheelchair to the elevator as I was leaving and he waved to me as I left. I was happy that I had visited and vowed to return again. On a second visit the following week, I learned from the nurse that he had been discharged. I wondered if Charlotte had discovered I had been to visit him and so had decided to take him home.

I was still working for the Nova Scotia government as Director of Personnel, when the Department I was working for was reorganized and integrated with another Department. It was the third one since I had been there. New organization charts were drawn up and employees had to be re-interviewed for their positions. I was among those interviewed and I lost my position to the Director of Personnel for the other Department.

I was offered another position but declined and asked for a compensation package. I was extremely stressed and exhausted. I decided I needed a rest, and so put all my belongings in storage and spent the next three months in a cottage by a lake owned by my friend Betty and her husband.

The cottage didn't have a telephone or a television, but I entertained myself with an electric piano keyboard I had bought as something to temporarily replace my piano. Years ago, a friend had given me a harmonica and I had always wanted to learn to play it. Now was as good a time as any. My piano keyboard had a jukebox so I could listen to tunes instead of playing. I decided to use it as a way to play the harmonica along with it. I particularly loved one of the songs, "Oh Danny Boy", and played it over and over and over on the harmonica until I finally mastered it. Years later I would be shocked to discover that my father also played the harmonica, and the song he played most often was, "Oh Danny Boy"!

I could not stay in the cottage forever and had to find work to support myself. What were my options now? I could look for work anywhere I wanted to, and considered going back to Fort McMurray. I considered many things and places but could not decide.

Then one day a letter arrived from Mark. He had enclosed a photo and on it had written, "Here's Hoping." I read the long letter and saw that he was inviting me to go to Ottawa. He suggested that I could stay with him and his daughters while I was looking for work and that perhaps we could pursue our relationship to see where it would lead. I didn't reply right away so he phoned, asking if I had decided. It seemed like a good plan and certainly better than anything I had come up with so far. I agreed and Mark said he would come to Nova Scotia to travel back with me.

Before I left Nova Scotia, I wanted Mark to drive with me to my father's home in Centreville. He had been ill and so was confined to his bed. As we arrived, I saw his wife Charlotte working outside and approached her.

"Hello Charlotte," I greeted her somewhat apprehensively.

"Should I know you?"

"Why yes, you should. I'm Laura Gidney, your husband's daughter.

"Oh!" It really sounded like she was saying, "So what!"

"I'm leaving for Ottawa and wanted to see my father before I left."

"I'm afraid I can't let you do that!" She made no move to invite us into the house.

"What? Why not?" I wanted to see him so much, perhaps for the last time.

"He's not well, and I don't want you to upset him!"

I knew when I was defeated. Mark and I left. As it turned out, that would have been the last time I would ever have a chance to say my goodbyes to him.

We left for Ottawa in July 1994. I drove my car while Mark led the way on his motorcycle. He had brought CB radios so we had communication for the trip. We arrived in Ottawa on July 16th and I settled into Mark's home with him and his two daughters.

But were Christine and Lea ready to have another woman living in their house? They were still grieving over the loss of their mother and it was a difficult situation for them. I wanted to be their friend but there was bound to be resentment over me living with their father—and there was.

With my domestic nature, I began trying to put their house in order. I wanted to clean, and cook and organize. It was too much, too soon, for Christine and Lea, and many times we clashed.

My routine was far different than what they had become accustomed to. Living with just their dad meant riding their motorcycles, having friends in, watching movies and talking—all activities that bonded them with their father and made for a great laid-back kind of lifestyle. One I was not used to. I was at one end of the domestic scale and they were at the other; it seemed neither of us would budge. Mark found himself in the middle, not wanting to take sides. But they were learning to enjoy the great home-cooked meals. We were starting to understand each other a little better.

Christine and Lea were both intelligent and beautiful girls with many friends. They loved their dad dearly, as he did them. I knew that any man who was as kind to his daughters as he was to them, had to be a wonderful person.

It wasn't long before I applied for a position with the Federal Government and was hired with the Department of Human Resources. I would work with their Training Department and design and teach their programs.

I began to work with the "Persons With Disabilities" group and helped them establish their terms of reference. Each year I traveled with the group across Canada; from British Columbia to Newfoundland. I could certainly relate to "Persons With Disabilities" and had a lot of empathy with them.

I could draw on my own experiences.

One day I received a phone call from Carmen. "I just got a call from someone in Bear River who said they had seen Victor Gidney's obituary in the paper."

"What? Are you sure it is our father?" I was shocked, since I hadn't heard from any of my father's family about his death.

"Oh yeah, it's the right one. They even bothered to include our names in the obituary as surviving members of the family, although they spelled our names incorrectly. And he died a month ago so I guess he's buried by now!"

This confirmed for me just how much we were seen as a part of the Gidney family.

It was hurtful that no one had the courtesy to let us know.

At home I developed a list of "housecleaning" chores and asked everyone to assume tasks in order to make it easier on me while I was working. It was helpful and things did get done, although often begrudgingly. I was imposing on their laid-back lifestyle and the resentment was growing.

Mark and I wanted to continue our relationship so I decided I should get an apartment closer to work. He arrived every Friday evening and stayed until Sunday night.

Mark finally decided to retire from the federal government and we began to talk of leaving Ottawa and buying a home in Nova Scotia.

With a map of Nova Scotia, we identified areas we did not want to live in, and others that we would consider. We found Real Estate agents in three areas of the province. Using the Decision Analysis process that I had taught, we identified our Musts and our Wants in a home and forwarded that to the agents. We read Real Estate listings and identified some that we were interested in viewing. Appointments were scheduled and we drove to Nova Scotia.

In April 1997, after viewing approximately twenty homes, we finally arrived at a place on the South Shore in a little town called Logan's Corner. This was it! We just knew it! It felt so right, and so we made an offer on the property before we returned to Ottawa. The sellers counter-offered and our second offer was successful. Hallelujah! This was to be our "home sweet home".

Chapter Fourteen

Life at Logan's Corner

On a second trip to Nova Scotia in June 1997 we signed the agreement to purchase. We assumed ownership of the house and were to move there in September. It was to be our retirement home and it was perfect.

Our property was 40 acres including many Christmas trees. It had a passable road into the woods. Although the front yard had been landscaped, we had a lot of work to do on the backyard.

We attended the Logan's Corner Baptist church. People there were curious as to who we were, where we came from, and why we decided to move to this community.

Neighbors arrived for visits. An elderly couple arrived with a basket containing raisin bread and fruit. The minister visited. We were made to feel welcome.

Before long I was asked to take over the "Praying Puppets" youth group at the church. I had been hoping to be asked to play the piano on occasion; however, it seemed they did not need my services.

We were to become "CFAs". CFA is a term used to describe "Come From Away". If you weren't an original member of this community or had direct ties to anyone who was, you were a CFA. Long-time residents had extended families close by and it seemed that everyone was someone else's "cousin". Such is life in a small community.

To my surprise I learned that I had an aunt who lived close by. I had not known my father's sister and knew her by name only, although she had seen me when I was a little girl. I contacted her and Mark and I visited her home. My Aunt Mary welcomed me and we immediately felt like family. Mary had recently been diagnosed with cancer and was not well. Unfortunately our time together would only last for three months until she passed away. I was happy to have been able to spend some time with her; I felt that I had some connection to the community.

I attended Aunt Mary's funeral at the Logan's Corner Baptist Church and it seemed so strange that I was sitting with the Gidney family, my father's relatives. My father's widow Charlotte sat behind me and wanted to know who I was! I was taken aback when outside she approached me, and said, "I'm so sorry that you weren't able to attend your father's funeral." I smiled, but said nothing. I wanted to say, "I would have if anyone had bothered to let me know!"

Mark and I each established a small business. Mark started "Best Christmas Trees", and I started LJE Consulting. Our major purchases included an ATV, a ride-on lawn tractor and numerous tools for Mark to shear our Christmas trees. We also bought a video camera so we could record our many experiences, the first of which was our adventure getting our first Christmas tree on our own property.

I obtained contracts from the Federal Government to work with the "Persons With Disabilities" committee, and traveled across Canada with them. Writing a "Persons with Disabilities" training manual was a project I could do from home; it paid $5,000. I flew to Ottawa to teach potential trainers how to use the program.

Mark was working hard at learning to shear trees; it was harder work than he had anticipated but he enjoyed it. He laughingly said, "The second year I doubled my business." The first year he sold one tree and the next year two!

Soon our home included "Jordan", our beautiful Doberman. I had always been afraid of Dobermans, but Jordan showed me her loving nature and I fell in love. She was my girl and I felt like a mother again. Jordan developed hip dysplasia as many Dobermans seem to, but she continued to run about as though she was training for the Olympics.

We were at the Veterinary Clinic when I noticed an ad: "Purebred Yellow Lab to give away to a good home." I told Mark "I just want to look"; he knew better but we went anyway. One look at "Mickey" and he was mine! He would be wonderful company for Jordan. They immediately became bosom buddies and it was amazing to watch the way they communicated with each other through nudges and play bites.

Mark and I were in town one day and as usual had Jordan and Mickey with us. A scruffy old man passing by noticed our dogs and commented, "I got a big dog I'll give ya!" He seemed quite "rough around the edges" and I wondered whether anyone who would just offer their dog to a stranger

138

as if he didn't care two hoots about him was capable of treating the dog as he should. I was on a rescue mission and asked Mark to get the man's name and tell him that we would like to go and see the dog. We arrived at the man's house to see "Sam", a huge Doberman who was tied by a big rusty chain in a junkyard of old cars. Sam didn't seem to have any access to water. When I asked if Sam was always tied, he said, "Sometimes I put him in the garage to guard my car." The inside of the garage was only big enough to hold the car and just room enough for the dog to squeeze around. I had seen enough! Sam appeared to be a big vicious dog, but I knew he was just heart-broken. I knelt in front of him and he came to me immediately. He knew I wasn't afraid and meant him no harm. Sam was going home with us!

Mark asked me if I "wanted to think about it". My answer was, "Put him in the car!" Sam was going to his new home where he would not be tied and where he would have more love than he had ever had before. And he did. Now Jordan and Mickey had another playmate. For a long time though, Sam just walked in circles; probably because all the freedom he had ever known was walking in circles around a car in the garage. Soon he was joining the others running through our fields like a wild horse. I knew if he could talk he would have said, "Thank You."

I was away from home working on a contract and Mark met me at the airport on my return. He greeted me with some sad news. Sam had been struck on the highway by a van and was in the Animal Hospital for surgery.

Sam had a steel rod inserted in his front leg and shoulder and was in a cast. We brought him home and he was given the privilege of lying on the couch with a pillow and comforter. His body recovered but his disposition had changed. He and I still played and I never feared him but we couldn't be sure how he would react to anyone else.

I was still on my mission to rescue all dogs. Perhaps I was relating to being abused and knew what it felt like not to have a home and be loved. Perhaps I had never forgotten the time, years ago, when I had seen Clarence take out his frustrations with me on our poor innocent dog. Maybe I was trying to make amends for that hurt.

I was attending the regular Sunday flea market in Bridgewater Mall when I saw a small black lab puppy no more than six or eight weeks old. He had huge paws for his size and was sitting on a bench with a big sign around his neck: "FOR SALE". The woman holding the dog said, "I ain't going to take him home!" She was going to sell him by hook or by crook. Of course I sat on the bench with her and held the puppy on my lap. I was hooked! But what would Mark say? I'd just have to worry about that when I got home, wouldn't I? Fifty dollars left my purse and the little puppy was safe. He was going home with me! And so he did. I knew that Mark once had a dog named "Shadow" who had died, so I decided that when I arrived home, the puppy would be introduced as "Shadow"—that was bound to influence Mark's reaction! Thankfully Mark was becoming as much of a "dog rescuer" as I was, and so Shadow became part of our Animal Kingdom. He was adorable as he scampered around jumping and tormenting the other dogs. Somehow they all accepted him as we did. Now we had four dogs; and did I mention two cats?

Sam was becoming very protective of me and snarled at Mark when he came near. He was becoming more of a threat to Mark than we could allow and so we consulted our veterinarian who advised us that Sam may be in pain as a result of his broken bones and he would probably become progressively aggressive. I did not want to face the thought of putting Sam to sleep but we could not accept the possibility of Mark being attacked. We reached a decision and sobbed openly as Sam was injected. An animal lover must face their heart being broken in many pieces over and over again. I was sick and many times questioned the decision.

Jordan began to lose the co-ordination in her back legs. We took her for acupuncture treatments but it didn't seem to help. One day I discovered that a large swelling had appeared on one of her front paws and suspected she might have somehow hurt it when she was running. It was much more serious, as the test results showed. The veterinarian said she had a tumor and so surgery was scheduled to remove it. She never walked again. She had cancer and it was progressing rapidly. She could no longer stand to go outside to use the bathroom and so I purchased adult diapers for her. Mark built a crib and I padded the sides and bottom with soft quilted padding. I covered her with a special quilt to keep her warm and cozy, and lay beside her for comfort. I kept offering her water and food but she would not eat. I offered her a plate of meatloaf, mashed potatoes and carrots. She became alert and gobbled the meal ravenously—and that was her last food. I could not accept that she would so soon leave us. I did not want to lose my precious Jordan. But we knew that Jordan was deteriorating quickly and did not want her to suffer. We made an appointment to have her "put to sleep." I bathed her and told her how much I loved her and dreaded taking her to the vet for the appointment that day. Mark put her bed in the back of our van and I covered her to keep her warm. The vet was kind enough to enter the van for the injection; she said, "Sleep well Sweetheart," and Jordan was gone.

We brought her body home and although it was November and the ground was frozen, Mark managed to dig a grave under one of our apple trees where she liked to play. He lined her resting place with fir tree boughs. We wrapped her in a green and white quilt and, through tears, Mark laid her down. Beside her head we placed an angel and one of her favourite doggie cookies. I left as I couldn't bear to see her covered with dirt. Mark made her a beautiful headstone and carved her name, the date, and her favourites: a squirrel and dog bone.

In tears that day, I wrote a poem for her called "A Part of My Heart".

Chapter Fifteen

New Life, Same Old Mom!

I enjoyed attending auctions wherever and whenever I could and often came home with the van full of cherished buys. Antique chairs, pump organ, depression glass, and tools for Mark. An old Pepsi wagon was a super find at $10. Mark could use it all the time to transport garbage to the roadside.

I became actively involved in the community and co-chaired the "Olden Days Festival" at the Dalewood Museum, with Louise DeLong.

Louise and I would become the greatest of friends after that. She knew very little about my past except that I had three daughters; yet she never pried. She accepted me as I was and for that I was grateful.

Louise encouraged me to start a Fashions shop and so I did and called it "Olden Days." The shop was located in a part of the large DeLong home. We had so many fun times there but finally it did not seem worthwhile financially and so I decided to close it.

One of Louise's hobbies was genealogy. She phoned one day and was so excited, telling me she had discovered that my grandfather Derline had been a first cousin to the man who had built and lived in the house we now lived in! Did that explain why I had felt such a connection to the house right from the beginning? Was it fate?

I also served on the Board of Directors for the Medical Centre; three years as President.

Every week I played the piano or the organ for the residents of a nursing home in our village. I gained a new awareness of what it was like to be elderly and in need of care.

The Women's Institute met monthly in Logan's Corner and I attended regularly, serving as President for a year. We had many fun times and laughs together. I was their "official comedian" and many times was put in charge of their entertainment.

I was also on the Board of Directors for the Dalewood Museum.

It was beginning to feel like I had no time for any "retirement" and that I was still working full time. There were so many other things I wanted to do at home but had no time. I was becoming exhausted and made a decision to withdraw from community activities, at least for the time being.

My mother was living in Bear River during this time and I frequently received phone calls from her complaining about where she was living. She didn't like the place, the food, or the people. "What am I going to do?" she asked. I agreed to go to see her and assess the situation. I told her I would try to find her a place close to where I lived. I brought her back with me for a visit. The first thing she did was to complain about the steps to get into the house although there was only one. She complained about the one step leading from the living room down into the dining room: "Why didn't you tell me?" Within a couple of weeks, my friend Betty and I packed all her things and moved her to Logan's Corner with Mark and I, while I searched for a place where she would be well cared for.

I was still working with my Consulting business and frequently had to travel across Canada, so staying with us was not an option. Mom was not pleased that she couldn't live with us and I was made to feel guilty. A place was recommended by a friend with an Ehrlichmann family where they took in senior boarders. I visited the place and spoke to Mrs. Ehrlichmann. She had a vacant room and was prepared to have Mom go live there; her rent would be $700 a month. It seemed a good idea at the time, but it proved to be an irony that the German origin and meaning of "Ehrlichmann" was "honest man." I would be close by and able to visit her and do whatever errands she needed.

I visited Mom frequently, and always brought along homemade goodies like apple pie, desserts, and her favourite candies. Since the Ehrlichmanns were Jehovah Witnesses and didn't celebrate Christmas, I would take a little decorated tree for her room, and gifts for her to open; a watch with large numbers, a tape player with tapes, housecoat, nightgowns and other clothes. Nothing seemed to please her and she particularly chastised me for bringing a Christmas tree: "What were you thinking? They are Jehovah Witnesses!"

Mom never got outside of the house except to keep a doctor's appointment or to visit our home, so when she wanted a new sweater I took her for a drive to the Mall. I got a wheelchair and wheeled her into the stores to pick out her own. She complained constantly: "Why are you doing this to me?" and "Don't you know that I can't do this!" Against her protests, we found a sweater anyway. It was probably the first time she had been anywhere in years. I had thought she would enjoy the change, but I was wrong.

I brought her to our house for visits, and Mark and I would try to make her welcome and comfortable. She always seemed bitter rather than thankful for our efforts. It was the same old story—nothing pleased her.

At Mom's request I looked after all her financial affairs, setting up a joint account at our local bank and transferring $20,000.00 into it from her bank in Bear River. Her pension cheques would continue to be deposited to her Bear River account. I kept $100.00 cash on hand for whatever miscellaneous items Mom wanted. I also kept receipts judiciously and never spent a cent of her money unless she requested it. She was continually asking me how much money she had and I was continually reviewing this with her. She either didn't understand or was simply testing me to see if my story changed.

She wanted a will prepared, and so my daughter Elizabeth who was now a lawyer prepared one for her. It was signed and witnessed by the Ehrlichmanns.

A few months later, I had a chance to go to the Dominican Republic for a week with Elizabeth. Her firm was paying for their employee's trip and would cover half of the cost for a guest. I was excited about the trip and told Mom that I would be away for a week. Before I left I made sure she had her prescriptions filled and made trips to town to find her comfortable slippers and whatever other errands she needed.

When I returned home Mark told me that while I was gone, my mother had phoned and told him she wanted her financial files. He took them to her, and she told him, "I am changing my will and leaving everything to the Ehrlichmanns." Mark asked her why she would do this and she replied, "Because they made me an offer I couldn't refuse."

The bank phoned me to say that Mom had withdrawn all the money from the joint account and thought I should be informed. I was surprised and angry that she would do such a thing so suddenly, and especially during the short time that I was away.

I decided to pay a visit to the Ehrlichmanns to see what had happened and why. Mark came with me. Mrs. Ehrlichmann met me at the door and was soon invisible though obviously listening from the kitchen. Mark and I entered the living room where my mother was sitting. I asked her what was going on. She looked very indignant as usual and said, "I changed my will." I asked her why. She told me "That's what I wanted to do." She was going to stay there until she died and the Ehrlichmanns had agreed to care for her until she died, in exchange for her estate.

I had only been away for a week, but the opportunity seemed to have presented itself for the Ehrlichmanns to arrange for a lawyer to prepare a new will, and a doctor to certify that she was mentally competent. They seemed to have covered all the bases very quickly before I returned. It seemed there was nothing I could do as they had also managed to get my mother's Power of Attorney. I discovered the meaning of *sneaky*! My mother had managed to accumulate $70,000 and the Ehrlichmanns wanted it. Not that they were poor; they owned considerable land throughout the village and operated a thriving business. The money meant nothing to me, but the fact that I had absolutely no control over my mother's future welfare or health needs angered me beyond belief. I was her daughter and the only family she had left, but she had totally disregarded that fact.

I spoke my piece and we left, but not before my mother referred to Mark as "That". Mark turned to her and said, "I don't know why, but she loves you. You are going to die a lonely old woman with no one around you who cares." It felt like a funeral and I had dressed appropriately in black. There was nothing more I could do but leave.

I had visited Mom at the Ehrlichmanns regularly, taking photos, gifts, and treats for her. I had done her errands. I had organized and managed her paperwork faithfully. I had sat and talked with her. None of that was likely to happen again since my visiting her at the Ehrlichmanns was a thing of the past.

Within a few days, Mr. Ehrlichmann appeared at our door and asked to come inside. He proceeded to go on at length about how he thought "the devil was in her". He was referring to Mom. He was trying to absolve himself from any wrongdoing as no doubt must be required from any good Jehovah Witness. He failed miserably in our opinion and after going on at length and making absolutely no sense, he left.

A year later, on Christmas Eve, my mother phoned and wanted me to go and get her from the Ehrlichmanns. "I hate it here!" she said. I was not about to set myself up for more heartache and told her I wouldn't. She had managed to dampen my Christmas Spirit.

Nevertheless I felt guilty about not being on good terms with my mother although this had been a life-long problem. I was haunted by the commandment to "Honour Thy Father and Thy Mother", and I decided to brace myself and pay her a visit. Mom was in bed and she looked a hundred years old! No teeth, no glasses, and now she couldn't walk. A wheelchair was crammed into her small bedroom and beside her bed was a chair with her pot underneath. She was in diapers! For the first time in my life the fear I had of her changed to pity. She was helpless and couldn't hurt me any more—or so I thought. I asked her why she didn't have any teeth or glasses.

It became very clear that Mrs. Ehrlichmann had been eavesdropping since she entered the bedroom right away to try and explain away why Mom didn't have teeth or glasses. It didn't make sense and it seemed to me that they didn't want to dip into the money Mom had given them. I had no choice but to be civil with her as she could easily refuse to let me in the house. Once again, I felt helpless to do anything.

As I passed through the kitchen to exit I saw how Mrs. Ehrlichmann could eavesdrop. There was a speaker system set up and amplified any sound from my mother's bedroom.

I decided to visit Mom frequently and each time Mrs. Ehrlichmann hovered. She was nervous about anything I might find out. It did seem strange that all of a sudden now Mom had teeth and glasses.

I visited my mother as often as I could and would sit on her bed and try to talk to her. She recognized me but seemed confused and asked about her sister Margaret, who had died. Always Mrs. Ehrlichmann would eavesdrop and hover. She seemed nervous when I was there, no doubt afraid that Mom would say something she didn't want her to.

Then in March 2004, I had my regular annual check-up. At Mark's prompting, since I was still smoking, I asked for a chest X-ray. My doctor phoned the next day and asked me to meet with her to discuss the results.

"The X-ray showed a shadowing on the left lung so I have scheduled a CAT scan for you," the doctor told me. "There is a possibility that it could be cancer but we won't know until the results come back. But don't worry, it could be nothing!"

Like everyone, I had always dreaded hearing the "C"-word—"cancer!"

A CAT scan revealed that there was indeed a tumor. It was hiding behind my liver but it was not on the left lung, it was on my right lung! Something they could not have discovered with the X-Ray. That discovery had to be divine intervention.

The surgeon in Halifax was confident it was in fact cancer, and decided that aggressive surgery was the solution. Within a month I was admitted to the hospital and the bottom lobe of my right lung was removed.

Being connected to a machine by a long tube inserted into my lung was far from pleasant and made it difficult to be mobile. Yet they insisted I walk up and down the halls, over and over again. I was overwhelmed with nausea—the old familiar feeling of being pregnant. I was so homesick and was anxious to leave the hospital and return to "safety." I was worried I might never see home again. "Oh please, Lord," I prayed, "help me to recover quickly."

I was unnerved one day when I heard a "hissssssssss" coming from the tube inserted in my lung. What was it?

And now there was fluid leaking and the bed was becoming wet! Frantically searching for the cause, I discovered that the hose had come apart from the tape they had used to secure it. I quickly resealed the break using the old piece of tape and the hissing stopped. What if I had been asleep? The machine assisted my breathing and I shuddered to think what might have happened.

Finally the day arrived when my doctor said I was well enough to go home.

Mark had expected that I would require constant care, but on my first day at home I surprised him by getting up and making breakfast. I had been so afraid that I would never see home again.

Chapter Sixteen

At the End of the Rainbow

On August 2, 2004, Mark and I were married in an outdoor wedding in the backyard of our wonderful home.

We had decided to put our money into landscaping the grounds for our wedding, instead of spending the money on a wedding and reception elsewhere. That way we would reap the longer-term benefits.

We hired a landscaper to create beautiful flower gardens. The place came alive with colour everywhere, including the island in our pond, and a trellis through which the wedding party would enter. Numerous chimes were hung throughout the trees and created an atmosphere of magic.

Mark and I were so delighted that all of our children and grandchildren were able to attend; my daughter Lisa, and son Spencer; daughter Julie, son Alan, and daughter Lila; Elizabeth; and Mark's daughters Christine (expecting her first child) and daughter Lea. It was the first time all of them had been together and now our daughters would be stepsisters.

Guests had been mingling and enjoying the gardens, but were now taking their seats to prepare for the ceremony.

Musicians began playing beautiful songs like "What a Wonderful World", "Here We Stand" and "Through the Eyes of Love".

On that beautiful summer day standing under our prickly pear tree, Rev. Muller, resplendent in his clergy robes, stood waiting to join us in "Holy Matrimony". Mark and his Best Man were dressed in their tuxedos, and waited with him for the ceremony to begin.

Our cherished labs, Mickey and Shadow, who had been professionally groomed and dressed in black bow ties, were led by grandson Spencer, as they entered through the trellis to signal the arrival of the bridal party.

Musicians played "The Bridal March" as my adorable little grand-daughter dressed in "Flower Girl finery" held hands with her companion who sported a mini top hat and carried the wedding rings on a lace pillow.

My sister Carmen followed, walking elegantly and looking as glamourous as any Bridesmaid had ever looked.

I entered through the rose-decorated trellis to approach my sweetheart, the man of my dreams.

"You're beautiful!" Mark said as took my hand.

As we gazed lovingly into each other's eyes, Mark and I exchanged vows.

Rev. Muller smiled broadly as he pronounced us man and wife and introduced us to the guests as "Mr. and Mrs. Mark Warren."

Each wedding anniversary Mark and I hold a private celebration under the prickly pear tree. We say what we appreciate and love about each other, and renew our commitment.

A month after we were married, I received a call from Mrs. Ehrlichmann to say my mother had died. If I wanted to see her, her body was at the Bridgewater Hospital. I phoned my sister Carmen and we met there for one last look at the person who had been our mother.

We watched for our mother's obituary but the Ehrlichmanns had not bothered to put one in the papers. There was no funeral. The Ehrlichmanns had Power of Attorney and I had absolutely no say in any arrangements.

Mr. Ehrlichmann arrived somewhat sheepishly at our door to deliver a copy of the will. Our mother had left Carmen and I each $10.00—yes, ten dollars! I still have the cheque. The will left everything to the Ehrlichmanns, including her personal effects. I didn't care about the money (something in excess of $70,000), but not being able to have my mother's personal effects was a slap in the face. I had given her so many gifts, and photos; a special one of Grammy Lil which I cherished, and some of her grandchildren and great-grandchildren which I would have loved to keep. The Ehrlichmanns now had everything she owned; including her rings and her memories and they made no effort to pass any of those to me or my sister. I knew that Mom had prepaid her funeral and that she would be buried with her husband "Mac" MacGregor in Digby, Nova Scotia.

♣

I had always suspected that my diagnosis of "polio" had in fact been the result of abuse; perhaps a blow to my head? My mother had simply *told me* that I had polio, but she had always avoided telling me any details of the experience. I could never recall the doctors or nurses using *that* word; but I was only two years old at the time. I decided to look into my health records and after lengthy research, my suspicions were confirmed.

The medical records showed that I had "suffered Growth Plate Injury due to trauma". Orthopaedic surgery had been required.

A growth plate is the portion of our bone that grows as children age. The growth plate generally consists of cartilage that will gradually harden into bone. Growth plate injury can be caused by trauma, which can lead to bone deformities, and even stop bone growth altogether. Treatment for a simple injured growth plate can be rest, protection and immobilization, but orthopaedic surgery may be needed to lengthen/shorten, re-align or otherwise correct abnormal growth plates.

I had lived all my life thinking I had polio. I thought of all those years of not being able to walk like others, not being able to play sports, not being able to wear the clothes and shoes I wanted to, all the pain and embarrassment of wearing orthopaedic shoes, all those years of looking in the mirror and wishing I had two legs the same size, all the pain and discomfort from the operations I had! And why?

Because my mother hit me in a rage? All the evasiveness whenever I asked my aunts and grandmother questions about my "polio" came to mind. Now I knew the truth! Mom had died thinking I would never know. I still loved her but I couldn't shed a tear.

That part of my life was over now.

EPILOGUE

Sunshine after the Storms

I have always hidden my heartaches "Behind the Smile". Now I know a broken heart can mend, if it finds love. Now I have something to smile about.

Mark is the kindest and most loyal husband any woman could ever want. We love our "Home Sweet Home" and never want to leave here. We are devoted to our "Animal Kingdom". They give us unconditional love, which we happily return.

Christmas at our house is always a time of peace and joy, a time to celebrate the true meaning of Christmas.

My greatest accomplishment in life has been to give birth to my three daughters; the sweetest and most wonderful girls in the world. We spend time together as often as possible, and I cherish the times with them and my grandchildren. They have brought such great joy to my life.

My regular cancer checkups have all been good news. It was four years ago in April 2008 and it is now reaching the magic five-year cancer-free mark. Life is too great to be cut short now, and Mark says, "He needs me!"

Whatever our future holds, we will approach it hand in hand, together.

We can't imagine life without each other now, and are thankful we are so in love in our Golden Years.

God has indeed saved the best for last for me. Each day is a blessing and I pray for many more until I'm safe "In the Arms of the Angels".

Behind the Smile

Behind the smile a terror hides
Of losing every step she climbs.

She climbed but fell one time before
Now nothing's safe, nor feels secure.

She smiles and thinks of days gone by,
Thoughts of her children make her cry.

She is without all she once had
But smiles to hide her life so sad

Then Hope calls as He passes by:
"Fear not, child, it is I."

About the Author

Born in Nova Scotia, Dianne Nice worked for many years in Management training. She is now retired to a large property in rural Nova Scotia where she and her husband devote their time to the protection of animals and pursuing their ambitions in writing.... and each other.